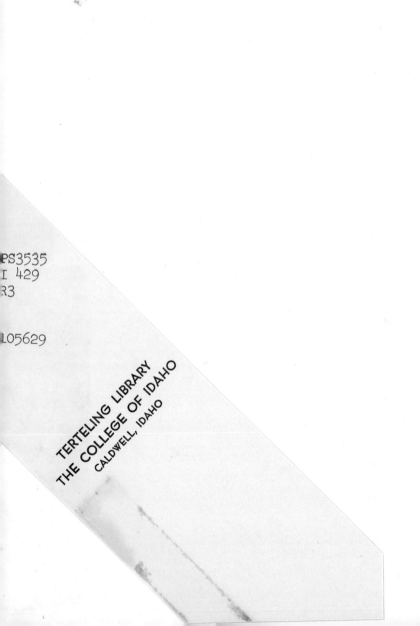

ALSO BY CONRAD RICHTER

THESE ARE BORZOI BOOKS, PUBLISHED IN NEW YORK
BY ALFRED A. KNOPF

The Rawhide Knot
and Other Stories

THE
Rawhide Knot
AND
OTHER STORIES

by Conrad Richter

NEW YORK

ALFRED · A · KNOPF

1978

THIS IS A BORZOI BOOK
PUBLISHED BY ALFRED A. KNOPF, INC.

All of the stories in this book were first published in
the *Saturday Evening Post*: "The Simple Life," under
the title "Life Was Simple Then"; "The Iron Shrine,"
under the title "The Iron Lady"; "The Dower Chest,"
under the title "Last Man Alive."

Library of Congress Cataloging in Publication Data
Richter, Conrad, 1890–1968.
The rawhide knot and other stories.
CONTENTS: The rawhide knot.—Smoke over the
prairie.—The flood. [etc.]
I.   Western stories. I.   Title.
PZ3.R417Raw   1978   [PS3535.I429]
813' .5'2   78-1637
ISBN 0-394-50208-6

Published October 2, 1978
Second Printing, November 1978

Manufactured in the United States of America

Contents

———————

Foreword

W HEN MY FATHER, Conrad Richter, began his series
of pioneer stories for the *Saturday Evening Post,*
he probably never thought they would become classics of
the American frontier. But he did realize that in these brief
short stories were buried the shapes of novels, that their
enormous condensation captured not the historical past but
its living essence. In fact, the title story, "The Rawhide
Knot," which tells of the marriage and death of Sayward,
would later be expanded into the three books of *The Awakening Land.* Like the seed in the fruit, it contains the larger
outlines of the Ohio trilogy, the vigor, sweep, and humor.

This ability to compress the times and spaces of a
country into tight mythic structures was, I believe, unique.
At times it resembles the lost art of the ballad-maker. As in
the ballad, all but the essential is pared away; details are
significant, omissions tell volumes. The themes of endurance, of conflict between peoples, generations, or ways of
life, are universal. The emotional tone combines a sometimes harsh, sometimes gentle lament for times past with a
constant affirmation of life in the face of death and violence.

Even the cadence of the prose seems at times to belong
to the oral tradition. The voice of the story-teller, sure of his
rhythms, certain of his ability to bring the reader into the

tense golden circle of the tale, is present from the opening sentence. It flies ahead of the reader, drawing him on. The suspense, tied always to the sights, sounds, and smells of the living scene, is pulled taut.

Because of the suspense, the stories read quickly, with an almost elemental simplicity. But Conrad Richter's means of achieving this are complex—the problems of his craft, as he told a writer friend. The chief problems had to do with compression: not only how to contract a long-term drama into a short story, but pack in daily incident and authenticity so that it brims with life and reality. Some of the compression comes through swift pictures, like that of Bethiah "sitting there with a face white as gyp rock, in a bright red dress above those jetty-black oxen," or by broad panoramic scenes, crowded with motion like the frontier wedding dances, or empty as the distances seen by men on horseback with only "the black smear of buffalo" or "smoky herds of antelope floating like the shadow of a desert cloud across the prairie." Often a single image fuses two scenes, as when Laban noticed that his future bride's "breath caught up to his, chimed with it, and passed it, for all the world like the breathing of his father and mother in the beautiful red-cherry bed that had come from Kentucky in the wagons."

But there is another technique less easy to define, the creation of a vastness of time and space which, however compacted on the page, expands in the reader's mind. The boy in "Smoke Over the Prairie" tells himself after sunset that "five days' journey west across the territory the sun was still shining on flocks of my father's hundred thousand sheep," and he awakens in the darkness of the next morning imagining that sun already shining "a thousand miles

east on one of my father's mule or bull trains." A trail empty
because of Indian uprisings stretches three hundred miles to
the railroad. Indeed, in those days space was measured by
time: by several days' journey to the next settlement ("the
only fixed human habitation on a thousand square miles of
unfriendly prairie"), by the weeks spent painfully crawling
through woods and thickets from an Indian camp to white
country.

Seen sometimes through the eyes of a narrator, whose
awareness spans past and present, those distances are enhanced. The time frame not only enlarges the story, it filters
and gives it texture. The contrasts and tensions between
then and now increase. A new reality, one that has slipped
away "as if it might never have really been," emerges on the
level of legend or myth. Like a distillation, it is crystal clear.

The sense of this vastness of time/space came in part
from my father's move west in 1928. There were few paved
highways then in New Mexico. Rutted trails, passable
in the high-slung cars of the time, stretched to the horizon
with nothing more in sight than grazing cattle or a water
tank and windmill. Except for the ruin of the grasslands
through dirt-farming and drought, much of the West was as
it had been at the turn of the century.

And there were old-timers from as far back as the
1850's and '60's whose talk filled my father's notebooks with
incidents, characters, conversations. Listening to them, especially to one H. W. Hardy, a rancher and raconteur who
appears by name in "The Simple Life," he acquired that long-
lens view of those rude empires which were, he wrote in the
thirties, "here in America a little more than half a century
ago, and yet in another world and another age that was just

then—although we didn't know it—drawing to a violent close."

Violence runs through these stories. If the theme of marriage, "the rawhide knot," binds them roughly together as a collection, so do the cruelty and harshness of a new land. Marriage and death often come paired, as in "Early Americana," "The Dower Chest," or "The Flood." Circumstance forces strange unions, like that of the woodsy Sayward and the Bay State lawyer. The event is rarely romantic. When Juliana elopes with the railroad engineer in "Smoke Over the Prairie," it is a symbolic defiance of the patriarchal order.

That patriarchal image is strong: black-haired Frank Gant naked in his bath talking to an Apache chief; John Minor impassively drawing cards, knowing he might get the queen of hearts—representing his daughter, whom he must mercy-kill should the Comanches attack.

But more often it is the women who dominate the stories, who are stronger than the men who seek them. The frontier was not totally a man's world; women enjoyed an independence not theirs in civilized towns. Their scarcity enhanced their power. The feminine code was often more ruthless than the male's. In "The Iron Shrine," the secret of the ironmaster lies not in a hidden vein of ore but in the figure of his wife's mother whose brutal actions delivered him from his Indian captors.

The rough vigor of those characters reflects what Conrad Richter felt to be the discipline and challenge of the frontier—west or east—set against encroaching civilization. Yet the oppositions are more subtle. Frank Gant's struggle may not be so much against the corruption of the coming railroad as the blighting of his personal power. The religious pacifist is rescued by his pragmatic Jess who knows God saves those who save themselves. Doane Williams' reckless attempt to act out his role in a frontier feud is not stopped by other men—who perform as in a ritual—but by a chance of nature. Doane, fresh-faced, exuberant, given to telling lively stories, is hardly the typical "victim." But the circumstances of the near-tragedy give the story, humorous on the surface, a sober undercurrent.

The question of response to challenge, whether right or wrong, depends on the quality of that response. Those who endured on the frontier adapted, in often surprising and individual ways. This resilience fascinated my father, who saw in the human being a strength of resources which, paradoxically, could be aroused only by circumstances equally strong. Hardship seemed to create a breed of people not in existence today.

I remember once being taken with my father to a hidden box canyon in the Datil Mountains to see a herd of wild horses. The canyon, completely cut off, could be reached only by a rough trail. And when we first glimpsed the horses far away, then rushing past us in a thunder, they seemed a mythical breed. Certainly they were oblivious to the tamer role of the ranch horses outside, or the men who would later catch them. I think of my father's stories, and the people in them, as being like that herd of wild horses, coming from a world "slipped . . . out of reality now," but utterly unforgettable.

Albuquerque, New Mexico **HARVENA RICHTER**
March 1, 1978

The Rawhide Knot
and Other Stories

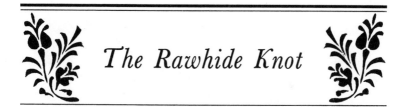

The Rawhide Knot

WITH HER DESCENDANTS GATHERED around her like the tribe of some pioneer matriarch in Genesis, Sayward Hewett Wheeler waited to see what would happen, for she had lived long enough and it was the Lord's move.

She lay in her massive walnut bed with a footboard broad enough to roll a wheelbarrow on and a headboard carved at the top like a squalling lynx, a very old woman with a great fleshless frame, almost bald, with no more color than the rusty liver spots in her dried-up cheeks, and her nose and chin like some formidable and bony vise that would catch and hold the devil himself if he meddled her way.

Tonight they had propped her up on the skids and trussing of her best goose-feather pillows like something that had just blown down the night before. Did they expect, she demanded of herself, that a gnarled and worn-out old apple tree could be propped up to take root in the earth again? Then she knew they didn't expect it at all. Two shapes under the Joseph's quilt on her bed caught her eye, and when she made them out they were her own legs, with no more life and feeling than a pair of rotted logs in the woods.

If the fools had only let her get up when she wanted to! Once she could have got out somewhere in the woods or a cornfield, she believed she could have tended to herself and been all right again. But the doctor, hurriedly sent for

3

by Victoria, begged her she must not give them any trouble. She was Mrs. Wheeler, widow of the great Portius Wheeler, whom Henry Clay had called the wheelhorse of the nation, and she was remembered as one of the most prominent women across the Ohio. She must realize that the rough life of the forest pioneers was over now. These were the modern days of the 1870's, and people didn't do those things any more. Oh, he was a very skilled and persuasive doctor, but it was plain he had never ridden a horse with the saddle straps of his medicine bags under his bottom or heard a wolf howl after him on the trace.

Sayward Hewett Wheeler knew well enough what he meant. The way people talked today, this was the golden age. The way they acted, it had been crude, even a little indelicate and uncivilized, to have lived seventy and eighty years ago, when she had. Most everybody now had boarded up their fireplaces. Few ladies smoked their pipes any more. Ministers declined grog. And if you said the word "petticoat" in front of anybody, they choked in the face like turkey cocks. Even the name of the settlement, Black Log, wasn't good enough for them any more, and they called the town Mount Huntington, God knows why, and tore down solid log landmarks to make way for three- and four-story buildings that shut out the sun, and gave themselves stylish airs generally as they came and went in a continuous, deafening confusion of arriving and departing stages, steam cars, carriages, hacks and drays.

And yet, the old woman told herself, with the saliva running furiously between her gums, if someone turned a hog loose on the streets of Mount Huntington, most of the people would still take after it.

She was aware of a shadow falling across the bed and a hand wiping the drool from among the long whitish hairs on her chin.

4

"Are you trying to tell us something, mamma?" Victoria's voice was raised against her ears as if she were deaf. "Is there something you want to say?"

Her mother tried to focus her bleary eyes on her daughter. So that's why they had crowded into this room tonight like an Indian scare at the blockhouse! Not as a mark of respect to a departing ancestor but to hear a deathbed confession or perhaps a last salty word of what a truthful old woman glimpsed of heaven.

"Yes," she heard her cracked old voice come out shrill and grim. "I got something I want to tell you."

She saw her son, Quincy, in the fashionable sideburns he had worn in Washington society, gazing at her with solemn and portly impressiveness, as if he could not have been the boy who had stolen his father's razor to shave off the bristles of the first young pig he butchered; and Mabry, long a leading banker of the state, coldly ready to repudiate his high-jump record in Union Township the day he tramped barefoot on two copperheads and a hoop, going for water through the wheat patch; and Ethan, who had been on the staff of General Rosecrans, standing at the door with his goatee and military bearing, as if he had never been the little tyke who used to whimper for her to go along outside with him in the dark before he climbed up to bed in the cabin loft.

Only Beriah would be different and down-to-earth, if her tired old eyes could find her. Her youngest and favorite granddaughter, Beriah, who, everybody said, looked like her. The one who wasn't married and wanted to go school-teaching out West, but the family had had a fit. It had put down its fashionable foot. No granddaughter of Portius Wheeler was going to go and probably get married to some uncouth Westerner who wore leather leggings like a savage and lived by himself in the wilds of some territory that

5

didn't even have a railroad. What would their distinguished ancestor have thought of that?

"You wanted to say something, mamma?" she heard Victoria prompt her.

The old woman muttered to herself grimly. So they didn't want anybody in the family with deerskin britches? It was high time she told them something about that—told Beriah too. If the room were a little lighter, her glazed old eyes might find her, but already the Lord was getting impatient and starting to turn down the oil lamps and stir ashes over the last few embers of the fire. She could barely make out Beriah's mother in a high, boned, net collar that reminded her of a picture she had once seen of a fancy silver fruit dish holding the head of John the Baptist, and across the footboard of her bed, three or four of her married lady granddaughters rigged out in puffs and fluting, and bows and ruching, and who stared at her now like the new settler lady from York state had gaped at Maw Jones when the Shawnees had scalped her.

That's what was the matter with the country, the old woman told herself angrily. Not politics like Portius had preached, but downright civilized refinement. All the fancy and cunning young hussies who jumped on chairs from a mouse and curled their hair over a lamp and screeched like a Wyandot when they bore a girl child no bigger'n a kitten could get themselves husbands—while a real woman like Beriah went a-begging.

The room was getting dimmer now, scarcely brighter than the glimmer of a rush light or her cabin grease lamp that, her father used to say, was steadier anyhow than a lightning bug. She felt the doctor's fingers tighten on her bony pulse, as if he could keep an old woman from going when her time was up! He turned his head and said something she couldn't understand for the growing wax in her ears. But the others heard and began to draw closer to the bed, until the old woman reminded herself that she had always been spry for a big woman and independent enough to take her leave before they pushed her.

Then unexpectedly she told the Lord he'd have to wait for a little. She had seen Beriah's head and shoulders above the others, a brawny girl, with a wide, good-humored mouth, coarse coppery hair like rusty flax, and bold cheekbones, that could bear man babies without a murmur. Standing there strong and unafraid, she was like a girl Sayward Hewett Wheeler had seen somewhere long ago by a dark stream, with the darker woods around her and the distant glow of a campfire like the faint red light of early morning breaking over her.

And suddenly the old woman knew it was herself, Saird Hewett, as the settlers called her, that she saw, in her short gown, with her hair in braids like the hawsers of a Monongahela keelboat, and life flowing through her, full and deep and broad-bellied as the Ohio.

The place had no more name than a wolf or a fisher, she told them in her old voice that had grown almost painfully shrill and was twanging with the pioneer dialect of her girlhood that had taken Portius twenty years to cure. The trees stood one agin the other all the way from Pennsylvania to the great English Lakes and the New Orleans River. Ever since her father's ox team had been ferried over the Ohio, the trace hadn't left them out of the deep woods any more than a mole out of his tunnel. Back in Pennsylvania had been day and night. Out here were only night and twilight. You could see by the sooty ground that it never saw a lick of the sun. Even God Almighty would have to take an ax to the high-handed, close-fisted timber if He wanted to see the firmament He made.

Stooping over the crick, she could hear the distant

whooping of drunken Indians from the post where trace and crick met. And when she came back in the firelight with the bucket of water on her arm, the stranger they had met at the post that day still held his log here by their fire, a solid-looking fellow in old tow britches, a linsey shirt and cowhide boots, and a white clay pipe sticking out of the furry black bearskin of his face.

He sat there listening to her father tell why he'd fetched a wagon along the trace sooner than an ark down the river. But his hands, like those of a man with more pressing business on his mind, kept cutting rings in a stick with a huge-bladed knife. And all the time Sayward felt his bright dark eyes watching her, as they had that afternoon when she had hitched herself up like a steer with the ox team and helped pull the mired wagon out of the crick.

"Is her married?" he asked suddenly.

"Her?" Sayward's father repeated, a little astonished, glancing involuntarily toward the black ringlets and milk-white face of his younger daughter, Genny, whom the boys had already begun to pester back in Pennsylvania.

"Her!" the bearded visitor said, pointing his knife, blade foremost, at the brawny figure of Sayward; and she felt a strange sensation, as if the blade had painlessly pierced a broad hidden breast.

Thomas Hewett stared stupidly at his eldest daughter. And by his face she guessed what he thought, as if he had blurted it out, which he was as liable as not to do, that this was the first time a man had ever so much as looked on his oldest girl. Back in Pennsylvania there hadn't been a boy she couldn't throw head over tin cup; but when it came to the girls these same boys walked home with after meeting, those were the fancy and cunning little wenches. Sometimes Thomas Hewett had pondered if a burly, hard-waisted girl like Sayward was not like the third sex of the bees that did the work and was neither male nor female.

8

Now he cleared his throat. "She's not married," was all he said.

"Is her promised then?" the other persisted.

"She's not promised that I knows of," Thomas Hewett said cautiously. His slow fingers brought out a leathern bag and started to fill his own pipe.

The caller put up his knife and leaned eagerly forward toward the girl's father.

"Look no further for a place to settle, then, stranger," he urged, and went on that south where he had his improvement was the finest cornland in the territory and a deed to the ground if a man were drafted to the wars. Already they had a thriving settlement of five cabins. All a settler needed for a crop was to clear a little land around the stumps, and all he, a bachelor, needed to clear his was a woman by his side like the other settlers had.

Thomas Hewett rose. In many ways he was self-willed and opinionated as a pignut hickory, but it was plain tonight that this was an unusual occasion and one not to be lightly dismissed, for a husband for his oldest girl had never happened before and might never happen again.

Sayward set down her bucket of water and stood there enigmatically composed as she saw her father half-face and silently interrogate her. It was in full sight and hearing of the stranger, but the latter had not spoken directly to Sayward on the subject and she would not to him.

"I'd 'a' told him about the old beaver dams ye seen around here when ye soldiered with Colonel Beauvais." She spoke in a strong, dispassionate yet positive tone. "I'd 'a' told him how the black land goes down to well water, and that's where ye aim to settle if ye can clear it."

"Oh, I can clear it my own self," her father said meaningly. "It might go a mite slower, but I can do it soon enough."

She gave her father a steady look, and now the hint of

9

harshness in her voice was, her mother used to say, the
Bowen blood talking. All the Bowens were strong as iron
and they had the iron rasp.

"I heerd ye tell the story so many times, about this bein'
the grandest country y'ever seen, I wouldn't want to stop
short of livin' here a spell myself."

The settler came over and spoke to her father in a low
tone, and her father spoke still lower to her, so the young
ones wouldn't hear.

"He says they's plenty of Shawnees and Delawares
around here to kill ye, but nary a decent white man to
marry ye."

Sayward stood there for perhaps a minute, a rooted
independent figure with the full light of the fire playing on
her thick rusty braids, her long shrewd hands and her
powerful legs that were bare to the knees.

"I'm obliged to him for speakin' for me," she said. Then
it could be seen that slow red spots had come to her cheekbones. "Ye can tell him he might be the first to ask me, but
he ain't the last."

Picking up her wooden bucket, she went to soak some
wash overnight on the dark side of the wagon.

When she came back she frowned at her younger sisters and brothers, peering out at her with a kind of surprised admiration through the wheels of the wagon under
which they had gone to bed—Achsa like a dark young squaw
rigged out in homespun, and Genny with her lady-white
hands that hated to touch a cow teat, and Sulie, the baby of
the family, the one they gave in to the most, and Michael,
who still slept with and was spoiled by his sisters.

Her father came over gruffly to the wagon, but she
could see the respect in his eyes.

"It stays cool in these woods. Ye better take the Joseph's
quilt for yer bed, if ye have a mind to."

The Rawhide Knot

Sayward did not say anything and she didn't open the chest in the wagon for the quilt of many colors. Dead and buried back in the cleared red soil of Pennsylvania, her mother still wouldn't like it taken out except for company or the preacher.

But the next time she waded in the crick to wash herself, she made out she'd take along a bar of Pennsylvania soap and scrub her young body with something more than soap grease and sand.

She was a woman now, she told herself, a white woman in this country of the men of the Western Waters, the vast northwestern territory of Ohio, the richest, blackest land in fifteen or twenty states and territories.

And when she lay down that night by the wagon wheel, with the fire lighting up the forest and the oxen and milk cows shoving their heads in a forest haycock Achsa had cut with the ax, she could see plain as her hand the other white men they had met at the post that day—Jake Tench, a big blacksmith in bloody buckskins who had jumped his bail from Kentucky and defied any sheriff's man to come and take him back; and George Roebuck, the trader, whose face was wrinkled and brown as if it had hung with the bear hams in the smoke loft; and a young unsociable yellow beard they called the Hermit, who had schooled at Yale to be a lawyer and lived alone in a bark hut in the forest.

The big Kentuckian had taken a fancy to little Michael and told some of the Shawnees to dance for him. And before they were done, a drunken Delaware with a nose like a musket stock had joined in, pantomiming, making grimaces ugly as sin, twisting his face this way and that, all the time dropping down on one knee and saying the same words in the Delaware talk.

"What does he say?" Achsa had asked.

"He say," a Shawnee had answered, "this way old white man from Kentucky look when he scalp'm."

The trader had hurried the young ones into the post, but Sayward had not gone too soon to miss seeing far back in the big Kentuckian's eyes a pair of murderous orange flames she had seen only once before, in a striking hawk's eyes.

And late that night when the carousing from the post had given out, she woke up with little Sulie clutching her with terror in her sleep and a distant scream dying through the forest, then all was still.

"A painter!" her father grunted, raising himself on one elbow to throw more wood on the fire.

But Sayward doubted if it had been a panther's scream. It sounded more like that of a savage tomahawked by a powerful Kentucky hand. Lying there with the soft breathing of her younger sisters and brother in her ears, she knew that this at last was the Western frontier they had come to, the Western border she had heard so much about. Back in Pennsylvania it had seemed as outlandish and far away as the Congo, where the blackamoors came from. It was a place she had never expected to see.

She told herself she was not scared of these men—not even of the big Kentuckian who never let the rifle out of his hands and who, the trader said, carried a razor strop he had tanned from a strip of Chief Cacusing's hide.

The only one she felt a little shy of was the yellow-bearded one who spoke to nobody except to the trader, and then only briefly, when he showed up at the post to pay a shilling postage on a letter that had never come.

Sayward told herself that a man was a fool to keep asking for a letter that never was writ. But she knew why he hardly spoke to anybody out here, not even to her. The way he looked at you and the straight way he walked minded her of the old Revolutioner, Captain Loudon, who stayed by himself with his blackamoor slaves in the brick house on the hill in Pennsylvania. Bigwigs used to come in fine coaches from Harrisburg and Philadelphia to stay with him. Once when she was a little sorrel-head, she had taken a kettle of huckleberries through the iron, gate, and had seen him in a blue coat, buff vest and breeches, and silver knee and shoe buckles.

Captain Loudon was old enough to be her grandfather. But the Hermit was a young man, no great shakes older than she was.

Before two years' trees had been cut and burned, there were four men Sayward knew she could have had if she had given a lick about having them—the furry-faced stranger she never saw again, and Jake Tench, whom she told she'd never marry on God's green earth any white savage who skinned a wolf alive to let it run; and the littlest settler she told she'd never marry a man who looked like Tom Thumb standing beside her; and Captain Charley in white men's trousers, the chief at Shawnee-town, who when she said no, drank up the fifty buckskins he had offered her father for her and came to the cabin that night making ugly signs, until she took his tomahawk away from him and tied him to a tree to sober up till morning.

All day now she could hear axes and saws raising a sociable hullabaloo there in the forest. Most of the settlers were Kentuckians and had come poling up the crick with their long rifles sticking out of one end of their boats and half-wild hogs sticking their snoots out of the other, and with steers or cows beaten by the young ones along the bank through the bushes. But a few had come on the trace with all their rattletraps on their back like a peddler.

And now, when someone reported seeing a panther and Sayward took the musket up the little ridge with the

young ones to listen for the cowbells, she could look down
on the young settlement of Black Log, and already it was like
a city, with twelve or fourteen cabins, not counting out-
houses, sending up their supper smoke within half a mile
of their nearest neighbor, with every house joined by deer
paths or at least blazed trees, and with all the cheerful
human sounds of women calling children from play in the
bush and of men bawling at their teams working late in
the new stumpy ground.

But when she turned her face the other way, where the
Hermit lived, all she could see were the lonely green waves
of unbroken forest that swallowed up his far hut like Jonah's
boat in the whale's belly. And all she could hear out there in
winter was the monotonous howling of the wolves.

The Kentuckians said it was a fitten place for a man
to hide. But Sayward told herself under her broad homespun bodice that a body was a fool to bury hisself alive just
because he didn't get a letter. It wasn't natural for a man
to live months on a string without seeing another human
face or hearing one of his own kind talking. Even the savages in the wilderness had their squaws and their savage
young ones.

Sayward hadn't seen the Hermit's youthful yellow
beard for many weeks now. She wondered today if she'd see
him at the marrying. All the people in the settlement had
gathered. Even George Roebuck had shut up his post. The
new squire had steel spectacles on and read the marriage
service out of his head as good as a preacher. And yet when
he said, "I pronounce ye man and wife," Sayward couldn't
feel any sweet pother inside of her.

Her mind kept straying, wondering what was to be in
this letter for the Hermit that had never come. Some said he
looked for a fortune, some for a pardon. But most believed
that if the letter came, it would come in a woman's handwrit-

ing. Sayward wondered who this woman might be and what she might be like, with her rings and her store scents and her whalebone stays.

Whoever she was, Sayward thought grimly, she better sharpen up a quill and write him his shilling letter soon. At first the settlers had talked of the Hermit with a backwoods pride for his young head full of book learning. But now they were poking fun at him, like the boys in Pennsylvania had hooted "Gypsy, tipsy!" after a wandering tinker until he threw stones.

All afternoon, talking under the trees or drinking sweetened brandy in wooden and pewter cups, or jigging it off in the house till the dust hung like a cloud over the dancers, the marrying stayed tame as a pet coon and flat as young ones' maple-sugar water, till Jake Tench, who was dancing a square four with Sayward, got a little free with her and she reached him an open brawny palm that caught him off balance and laid him partway to the floor. The first enthusiasm rose from the crowded log room, and Jake Tench joined in, going all the way to the floor and rolling himself like a log over the tamped dirt till he tumbled everybody at one end of the room in a scrambled, screeching heap.

He leaped, light as a catamount, to his feet.

"That's what's ailin' the settlement!" he sang out. "It's gettin' too hifalutin. Buildin' houses with hewed logs and riggin' up newfangled sweeps to grind yer corn fancy in a stump. Even a tradin' post ain't good enough for George any more and he calls it Roebuck's Grocery. And now Matt Chew had to get hisself squire papers and marry off John and Mariah, as if they hadn't been livin' peaceable together since her man got his hair lifted up in the Reserve."

Most of the women had their hands over their mouths to keep from laughing now. Jake Tench threw a look around, and Sayward saw the dancing black points in his eyes.

"What this settlement needs is a real marryin'," he told them. "With two turtle doves." Then he snatched the brandy jug from the bridegroom's fingers and legged it out of the door with most of the men and boys chasing after.

"Now look out for mischief!" cautioned Granny Wildermuth, who, as a bride in Kentucky, had killed an Indian with an ax.

And when Sayward looked out of the open door she could see Jake Tench jumping up and down, his heels clicking and his long black hair flinging, and the men were pushing one another in the ribs and pounding one another on the back, and some rolled on the ground.

Mrs. Jenner came hurrying in with her young one.

"They're hatchin' up another marryin'," she told them. "Jake Tench is fetchin' in the Hermit to Idy Tull's tonight to see if she'll have him."

Several women laughed out loud. Ida Tull, in her faded thirties, made a fuss as if she would swoon. But George Roebuck put on a sober mouth; and when Jake Tench came in to ask him for a keg of Monongahela from the post, the trader said resolutely he had no empty keg to spare. Nor had John Hocking any to lend.

"I can get ye a washtub, Jake," Bub Claflin offered.

Jake Tench waved him back recklessly. He stood there with the very devil sticking out of his eyes while Sayward saw a half-wild hog come grunting across the clearing.

"Will ye sell me that shoat, spot cash?" he mocked the bridegroom.

He tossed down a Mexican dollar, and when John Hocking couldn't resist picking it up, the big Kentuckian took out his long knife and with a triumphant yell flung himself on the squealing beast and killed it, skillfully skinning it whole, tying together the broken places and taking out the bone about two inches from the root of the tail, which served as the neck of his bottle.

The Rawhide Knot

Then, wiping his knife on his buckskins, he flung the hairy pigskin over his shoulder, pinned George Roebuck's arm forcibly in his and the two started for the post together, with the blacksmith calling back occasionally at the top of his voice that grew gradually mingled with the echoes rolling back from the forest, till it sounded like a pack of wild men, which, Sayward told herself, it was.

When he was gone, the women talked together in little bunches and Ida Tull carried on to all and any who would hear her, till Sayward quietly took Genny and Sulie and went on home, stomping in the head of a copperhead at Harbison's meadows, then taking off her shoes and letting down her hair to be comfortable on the road.

Behind her she was aware that Jake Tench had come back with his pigskin cask. She could hear the men whooping and carrying on from the Hocking cabin and, above them all, the wild voice of the blacksmith. Presently she heard them moving boisterously down the deer and cow path that led to the ridge and out in Hermit's Valley, singing, yelling, neighing, crowing and splitting themselves with laughter.

Sayward half-wished that her father was home this night instead of somewhere out on the trace freighting goods in his wagon for George Roebuck. She said nothing until the cows were pailed and they had downed their johnnycake and milk for supper. Then she sent Michael and Achsa, who could take care of herself with any man, over to build a small fire and wait at the foot of the Hermit's Valley path.

"When Jake Tench comes back, tell him I want to see him, drunk or sober," she told them.

The chipped-log cabin of the Hewetts was undaubed inside, for Genny said she wouldn't live next to mud. Seven rungs crossed the ladder instead of five, so little Sulie wouldn't fall through when she climbed to bed in the loft, of an evening. With his pocket compass Thomas Hewett had laid the cabin due north and south, plumb square with the earth itself. As for Sayward, plenty of the logs she had lifted with him to their notched place in the walls still bore the deep, unmistakable blade mark of her ax.

With her grease lamp on the bench in front of her and a candlestick hooked in a log, she was mending root tears in her shoes when she heard them coming back from Hermit's Valley. They were patting their hands to their mouths like Delawares. Little Sulie sat on her three-legged stool before the open door; and by the way the young one tightened, Sayward could tell when the men were close enough to see their torches through the trees.

Sayward did not look up. Her fingers kept pushing the needle through the tanned buckskin. At about the spot where Michael and Achsa had been sent to halt them, her ears told her that the men had turned down toward the cabin. And now that they were conscious of an audience, they barked and crowed and squealed like hogs and howled like wolves with the fresh, almost demented enthusiasm of a pack of squaws with a prisoner.

She could hear them breaking down her father's cornstalks as they came crowding along the path like cattle. The yellow flare from their bound hickory-bark torches licked through the open door and over the insides of the cabin till the chinked walls with their clapboard shelves and wooden pins hung with clothes were plainer than by day.

"Here I be, Saird Hewett, drunk or sober!" the voice of Jake Tench mocked her. "Turn out and see what we found in a hollow tree in Hermit's Valley."

Sayward coolly bit off her thread and slipped on her shoes. And at the doorway she told herself that all these men in home-plaited summer hats and wintry coonskin caps, in linsey and deerskin shirts, in tow and buckskin britches and in boots and homemade shoepacks, and some barefooted with their shoes tied around their necks, all dancing around, hollering and carrying on, reminded her of nothing so much as the Whig or Democrat parade her father had taken her to see as a tot in Pennsylvania. The men had worn steer heads and galloped around with cowtails tied on behind. At the time, she had never known that grown men could act so crazy. But if she had known them then as well as she knew them now, there was nothing she would have put past them.

"What'll ye bid for him to nigger logs, Saird?" Bill Losh yelled at her.

"Don't crowd him so close," Sayward told him angrily. "He ain't a greased hog."

The men in front pushed aside and Sayward looked down on the tall, defiant figure of the Hermit. She guessed they had had to hold him while they perked him up for the evening. His tawny beard was trimmed and a red ribbon tied around his gathered brown hair. Over his head likely they had pulled that shirt he must have brought from Boston or Maine. Their dirty fingers had marked it up as if a possum just out of the mud had tracked across it. But it was still white in spots and ruffled and of finer material than anything in the settlement, and it set off his deerskin britches.

His eyes were gray and bitter as they beat around, hunting a way of escape from his tormentors. And now and then when someone yanked him back in his place, they would burn till they reminded Sayward of Captain Loudon standing up with all the Revolutionary veterans around him to give the Independence Day oration.

With his long black hair swinging, Jake Tench jumped up to the doorway beside her, his rifle in his hands, a triumphant devilishness in his eyes.

"Allus takin' the side of dumb critters, ain't ye, Saird? Well, this time ye can't beat it. We're doin' the territory a favor addin' to the population. The Hermit and the old maid'll make a pair. She mought carry on for a while, but she'll take him. Come along and see them spliced."

For a moment Sayward stood, a rude, almost earthly

figure, her coppery hair bright in the flares, her full red skirts that were dyed with pokeberries filling the doorway.

"I'm not a-goin'," then she said calmly. "I'm a-stayin' and marryin' him my own self."

Jake Tench's black eyes contracted. "Yer wits is addled, Saird. Ye don't want a lazy good-for-nothin' like him around."

"He won't be a lazy good-for-nothin' around me," she said.

"They was a high-toned Boston woman he wanted to marry once," Jake told her brutally. "He don't want the likes of you."

"I'm still havin' him," Sayward said, "whether he wants to or no."

Jake Tench gave her a peculiar, reckless, almost admiring look. Then he wheeled and howled at the top of his voice: "Saird Hewett's a-willin' to take him her own self!"

The dancing and bobbing of the men stopped. Some cocked their heads for a little, unsure what to make of it. But when they glimpsed the Hermit staring up at Sayward in consternation, and when of a sudden he made a violent and unsuccessful attempt to escape, they whacked one another in the ribs and shoved one another sprawling and nearly split themselves laughing.

"Yer took, Saird!" Jake Tench roared at her. "Yer man's a-willin'! Come on and hoof yerself up to the squire's!"

"If the squire fetched himself to John Hocking's, he can fetch himself here," Sayward told him with dignity. "I'm a-gettin' married in my own cabin."

Holding lighted candles or burning sticks of dry shagbark like tapers, the women came through the dark woods and corn patches that night, laughing and calling to one another and crying out to Sayward, the minute they were in the cabin, what a sharp and a spry one she was and how nice she looked for her marrying with the fan breastpin on her bodice. Outside the men gathered wood for firelight and cavorted around like uncouth dancing bears, roaring out ribald songs and making the jocose admonitions of married men to the bridegroom.

Only when Jake Tench arrived with the squire and Billy Harbison with the pigskin cask on his shoulder freshly filled from the post did the men crowd boisterously inside.

Squire Chew's eyes had a furtive look behind his steel-bowed spectacles.

"Maybe ye'd ruther put off the marryin', Saird?" He cleared his throat. "Yer father's not here. Money's not plentiful. And I figure we ought to settle who's a-goin' to pay me beforehand."

"My father's got nothing to do with this," Sayward told him. "I got the small silver to pay ye."

"And the certificate with horses and parrot birds painted on it? That's extry."

"Me and him'll maul rails for ye for that," Sayward promised calmly.

The men shouted at the picture of the Hermit mauling fence rails. They promised him the loan of ax, maul, wedges and hair ribbons. They took his arm and jogged him up in front of the squire, where Sayward stood in her full red skirts, her rusty red hair and a red spot on each bold cheekbone. And when the squire, who owned no book, asked the bridegroom as he fancied it, "Do ye take this woman, Saird Hewett, as yer lawful wedded wife? Do ye promise to live with her in the holy act of matrimony, forsakin' all others for better or for worse so long as ye live? The answer is 'I do,'" they roared "He do!" till the oiled-paper windowpane rattled and shook like an oak leaf in March.

Standing there, from head to foot a picture of oaken calm, Sayward gave no indication that it mattered. And when the squire asked, "Saird Hewett, do ye take this man as your lawful wedded husband? Do ye promise to cleave to him and serve him, to comfort and help him through sickness and trouble till death does ye part? The answer is 'I do,'" she answered with such firm, quiet knowing-her-own-mind that the men sobered their mouths and hitched their neckbands, and some of the women paid that greatest compliment of dabbing at the eye with a corner of apron.

And then the squire solemnly declared them man and wife, there was a great hurrahing and carrying on, with the women fussing over Sayward and the men pumping the bridegroom's arm and slapping his back and dragging him over to the pigskin cask for a drink. And presently Jake Tench made a loud ado squaring off the cabin floor to dance, and shooing all the young ones up the ladder with Sulie and Michael to lie on their bellies and look down on the doings.

And from the loft it was an uproarious and never-to-be-forgotten night with the bright calicoes of the women moving among the dark trappings of the men, with the older girls whispering, giggling and snickering to themselves on one side of the downstairs bed and on the other side all the littlest ones laid together like baby coons in their hollow tree, with the rising smells of burning candles and dripping grog and haunches of venison turning on the fire, with the sounds of old man Steffy's fiddle and of men and women stomping the puncheons in the shuffle, the double shuffle, the half moon, the scamperdown and the Western fling, and rising with everything all the talk and chatter and laughing-fit-to-kill till the overflow of good spirits reached even the young ones on the loft and went to their heads like brandy, so that they kicked their heels and tickled their companions and rolled over wrestling and fighting till a Tull girl went headlong down the loft hole and for a minute the cabin was filled with her squalling.

"It's a sign," Granny Wildermuth predicted, "that Saird's and the Hermit's first young 'un'll be a gal."

The Rawhide Knot

Standing in a corner, the Hermit stiffened and paled, and made a sudden and violent bolt for the door, throwing even Jake Tench back against the clapboard shelves, fighting his weight in wildcats, astonishing them all till he reached the door and was gone in the night, leaving behind him only a cloth hat and a sorry rag from his ruffled shirt in somebody's fingers and half the guests doubled up with laughter.

"Get yer hounds!" Jake Tench called angrily to Billy Harbison.

"Let him go till ye eat," Sayward told them, bringing out white poplar chips to hold the refreshments.

"He won't stay out late for ye," the blacksmith said grimly. "We'll learn him he's a married man now."

It was after midnight and a thin moon hung over the lonesome black territory when the marrying frolic broke up. Genny and sleepy Sulie went home for the night with the Greers. Cora Wildermuth asked for Achsa, and the McFalls said they reckoned they could take Michael with their Hughy. Mrs. Harbison offered to stay and help Sayward redd up the cabin. She said her man wouldn't be home anyway till his hounds found the Hermit for the men that had gone out. But Sayward said she had nothing else to do her own self, not even to go home. And even if she had, it was her business to redd up after her own marrying.

The candles had burned out, but Sayward kept feeding the fire for light till under her long strong hands all signs of the frolic were gone, with the pewter in its place on the clapboard shelves and the puncheon floor clean enough to eat off of and the downstairs bed with the Joseph's quilt smoothed out from all them that had mussed it. The dust stirred up by the dancing had been wiped from the smooth logs, the hearth swept clean with a turkey wing and Jake Tench's empty pigskin hung on a walnut limb outside.

The moon was down somewhere in the black forest

when she heard them coming over the ridge. And when they reached the corn patch Jake Tench shot off his rifle to let her know, and the hounds bayed triumphantly at the sound of the powder.

"Nigh onto everybody must of gone home," she heard Billy Harbison's voice.

She couldn't hear what the others said. Then the door was pushed open and the brush-whipped, run-soaked and still defiant figure of the Hermit shoved across the threshold while the door slammed behind him and the men outside whistled and brayed and gobbled their enjoyment.

"Here yer bashful bridegroom be, Saird!" Jake Tench bellowed, in a voice meant to wake the dead.

Sayward said nothing. She could hear them, after a little, putting their ears to the door and like their eyes to cracks in the chinking.

"We'll set on yer step for ye, Saird," Jake Tench hollered, "and see he don't run off from ye till mornin'!"

Sayward got to her feet and opened the door.

"Ye're not settin' on my step, any of ye. Not on my marryin' night or any other night."

"What's got over ye, Saird?" the blacksmith complained. "After all we done for ye. Ye can't lock yer door that he can't open it hisself. The minute we uns go, he'll light off from ye like a redcoat."

"Then he can go his own self," Sayward told them. "I ain't a-holdin' him." A strong, calm figure, dependent on no one or nothing, she stood there in her freshly mended shoes and full red skirts, with the scrubbed, hand-split table she had set for one in plain sight, with pewter plate and fine bone-handled knife and fork and mug of brandy and the best cold victuals she could secretly put away for him.

She waited, but the Hermit made no movement to leave the cabin.

24

"He's broke to yer bed and board, Saird!" Jake Tench roared.

Like a young she-bear, Sayward turned on him. "Ye act like this was some kind of monkey marryin'!"

"Why, no, Saird," Jake Tench tried to smooth it over. "I was only stayin' around till ye'd talk him into lawyerin' a case for me, so I could go visitin' back to Kentuck."

"Well, ye can talk yer business when it's time for it, in the mornin'," she told them, and there was no mistaking the Bowen iron in her voice. "They was a painter screechin' and scratchin' around here last night. I give ye one and all fair warnin', the first screechin' and scratchin' around this cabin tonight, I aim to take the musket."

Then she closed the heavy door in their faces and whacked down the seasoned hickory bar. And after a while it was quiet and peaceful in the cabin, with the pleasant sight of a hungry man sitting up to the table and with the fire throwing its warm red light over the log walls and over the hand-split puncheons and the Joseph's quilt of many colors on the bed.

It was after daylight and blue smoke was rising from the chimney when Jake Tench came whistling through the Hewett corn patch. Sayward was up and dressed, patting johnnycake in front of the fire, and her husband buckling on his deerskin britches. Soaked last night in Panther Run, they had dried on the hearth till they felt as if, thrown to the floor, they would jangle like kettles. And when he pulled them on, it had been like getting into a pair of young, hollow trees.

"Is she all right to come in, Saird?" Jake Tench bellowed cautiously from the woodpile. "Did ye talk him into takin' my bail-jumpin' case?"

"He can make up his mind his own self," Sayward called back tartly. After a moment she saw her husband half-facing and silently interrogating her, much as her father had that night when the bear-faced suitor had popped the question. "He's yer first case in these parts," she told him in a low voice. "I'd make sure when I took him to lawyer him clear."

Then she called to Jake Tench to come in and talk it over with Portius Wheeler at breakfast, while she took the bucket out to pail the cows.

From the Albuquerque Enterprise, September 1, 1937.

MRS. BERIAH OVERLOCK, well over seventy years old, drove her car from the Overlock ranch in the Salado country to show modern young people how to dance a square dance at the Pioneers' Celebration here last night. Mrs. Overlock is the mother of Sen. Portius Overlock and came to New Mexico before the railroad. A big woman who likes to dance, she says, "There's nothing in the Bible against dancing."

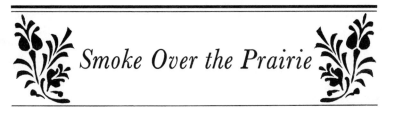

Smoke Over the Prairie

I<small>T IS GROUND INTO DUST</small> now like Mobeetie and Tascosa, swallowed up by the grass and desert along with split ox-shoes, shaggy buffalo trails, and the crude cap-and-ball rifle. And how can I say it so that you who were not there may see it as I did, rolling, surging, fermenting under the brazen territorial sun, that vanished rude empire of which my father was a baron, a land as feudal as old England, larger than the British Isles, with lords and freemen, savages and peons, most of them on horseback, all here in America a little more than half a century ago, and yet in another world and another age that was just then—although we didn't know it—drawing to a violent close?

I remember, as a small boy, climbing up our roof ladder in the shadowy blot after sunset and telling myself that five days' journey west across the territory the sun was still shining on flocks of my father's hundred thousand sheep. And I can remember the cavelike darkness of some early-morning waking between blankets tossed over tanned buffalo hides on my huge bed and thinking that a thousand miles east on one of my father's mule or bull trains the sun was already shining.

And today I would give a great deal just to glimpse that same sun warming the walls of my father's house, known from Fort Dodge to the Old Pueblo as Gant's Mansion, a squat palace of adobe standing on the San Blas plain, and to see again its wide hall trooping with a grave procession of princely territorial governors and hook-nosed judges, of Indian agents like blue-eyed foxes, of brass-buttoned Army officers, Federal officials, Mexican dons and *ricos*, and the hungry, grunting chiefs of the Utes, the Apaches and the Navajos.

But even then a cloud no bigger than your hand was beginning to cast a shadow over those adobe walls that stood thick enough to entomb horses. The smoke of the native cedar is blue and fragrant and melts into the air. This cloud on the eastern horizon was a smoke tamed by man, black, foreign, smelling of the pit, and had never hung over this wild land before.

I knew it was important that day my mother called to me in the hall. She sat massively in her armchair in her rooms, not a stout woman, but wrapped, even in summer, in shawls and overskirts, her eyes dark and bright like a bird's, in a quilted face which even then looked incredibly older than it was. All week I had been conscious of the clamp of her lip and the faint white spots, like touches of alkali, in my sister Juliana's cheeks.

"Go and ask your papa if he can spare the time from his business to talk to me," she said bitterly. "And you come with him."

I knew then that my father had not greeted her, although he had been back several hours from ten days among his sheep in the Canyon Bonito country. I had seen his dust-covered buggy pull up to the store, both horses lathered to the mane, as always when my father held the lines. I found him gone from the store, and I looked for him in his wholesale warehouses sprawling nearby, a kind of Ali Baba caves in barred windows, dim and odorous and heaped with inciting boxes, fat hogsheads, bulging bales, mountains of plump sacks, grain-bins, piles of hides to the roof, monstrous sacks of unwashed wool, and poisonous-looking copper ingots.

Smoke Over the Prairie

He wasn't there, and I went in turn to the clanging blacksmith shop, to the stables, where his late-driven horses stood in a kind of stupor, and to the wheelwright shop, choked with felloes and rims, blocks and shavings and the dismembered bodies of wagons that knew every ford and pitch hole on the Santa Fe trail.

Only one place remained where he might be, and I reproached myself that I hadn't gone there before—what we called the mansion office, a bare sweep of room with an adobe floor and little furniture except a battered desk whose drawers no one dared to touch. The place was empty, but a guttural of voices drifted from the bedroom beyond.

"Come in!" my father's voice called at my rap.

I lifted the iron latch and for an uncomfortable moment stood in the doorway.

A fire of *piñon* logs blazed in the bedroom fireplace, and on the floor with his back to it sat Guero, the Mescalero Apache chief, huge and greasy, with the eyes, nose and talons of an eagle, his red blanket thrown back from his shoulders, and bared in his rawhide belt a long American trade knife and the forbidden revolver.

And coolly talking to him from where he stood in a white bowl on the floor, washing himself from a second bowl on the marble top of the washstand, unclothed, unarmed, and unconcerned, stood my father, a powerful naked figure, not tall, but herculean, in a black beard that twisted and stood out from his chin and cheeks like fine wire. And I noticed that the same stubborn, black, invincible growth curled from his chest and the hard cylinders of his legs.

So far, he had not even glanced at the open door, and now he looked up with some impatience.

"Come in, come in!" he barked, and I stepped hastily into the room, dimly realizing that he had not known who was knocking, that it might have been one of the Mexican women servants with, perhaps, the governor and his lady behind her, but that my father did not care. His unforgettable eyes fixed themselves upon me. "You know Chief Guero," he commanded sternly. "Go up, shake hands and ask him in Spanish about his family."

When my father had pulled on clean linen and fresh black broadcloth, he summed up his long talk to Guero: "Tell your people this: Tell them there is no danger from the railroad. It will bring no white people here to take away your rights. It makes big promises. It talks big words. Today it boasts. Tomorrow it is forgotten."

He left Guero sitting on the earthen floor of the office, bent voraciously over a huge bowl of steaming mutton stew.

"Now," he said to me in the hall, "you say your mother wants to see me?" For a moment or two as he stood there he reminded me of the male blackbirds I had often seen in the tules, drawing in their brilliant scarlet shoulder-straps and soberly ruffling their feathers until their strut and sheen had vanished and they looked subdued and brown. Then I accompanied him in silence to my mother's door. He knocked and, without waiting for an answer, formally entered.

"Nettie!" He bowed gravely, and in that single word still in my ear I can detect greeting, irony, dignity, indulgence and uncomfortable expectation of what was to come.

My mother made no answer except the further clamp of her lip and the faint, unaccustomed rose in her cheeks. She motioned me to come and sit beside her, which I did, painfully conscious that it was an ignoble role I was to play, like the favorite child in *Ten Nights in a Barroom*, by whom the regeneration of the father was to be made.

My mother's quarters, which she seldom left, seemed perpetually compressed with a stale and heavy air, the musty scent of Eastern carpets, stuffed chests and ward-

robes, soaps, medicines and mothballs, all very distasteful
to a boy. But today I felt that the sluggish air had been
charged with sharp and potent currents. And when I looked
at the golden-brown shawl which hung like a vestment about
my mother's shoulders, there was almost the play of lightning upon it.

"Must I speak of it?" my mother began bitterly. "I should
think you'd confess it yourself with shame!"

No step was audible outside the door, but the latch
lifted and drew our eyes. Slowly the door opened. It was
Juliana. I can see her today, framed in that massive doorway with the light like a nimbus behind her, quiet, grave-
faced, a girlish figure in her full skirts and snug bodice,
both of them dove-colored, and over the latter the gold chain
and heart-shaped locket in which I knew she carried the picture of her father.

"John is here. Can't I stay?" she asked, and closed the
door. With the hushed step of a young woman late to
church, she crossed the room to a chair, and the appeal in
her eyes as for a moment she glanced up at my father might
almost have been at God.

My mother's eyes burned with maternal satisfaction
at Juliana's presence.

"People are saying," she went on scathingly to my
father, "that Mr. Rutherford has disappeared like other
enemies of the high-handed interests in this territory."

I fancied I saw a hidden stain through the beard on
my father's cheeks, and my mind traveled with a sort of
horror to Vance Rutherford, tall, fine-looking, and gentlemanly, whom Juliana had met at the Coddoms' in Capitan.
Up until the last ten days he had kept driving to the mansion
in a livery rig to pay her attentions, and I had wondered
what had become of his narrow-brim hat and the invariable
desert marigold in his buttonhole.

"People say many things, Nettie, many things," my father said.

"Is he dead?" my mother demanded in a blunt voice, and I saw the locket hang motionless for a moment on Juliana's breast.

"No-o," my father said blandly. "Not that I know of." And the locket resumed its silent rise and fall.

"Then you warned him to leave the territory?" my mother accused.

"I may have"—my father lifted a square hand—"seen that he heard certain discreet things."

"You had nothing against him, Frank Gant, except that he's chief engineer for the railroad!" my mother challenged hotly. "Where can you find another young man in such a high position? Do you want your daughter to marry a cowboy or buffalo hunter who rides and kills and gambles and soaks himself in the whisky you sell like coffee and sugar over your counters?"

My father prudently said nothing. The color gathered in my mother's face.

"You're prejudiced against the railroad! I say, thank God for the railroad. It's the finest thing that could happen to this lawless land. It will bring schools and churches."

"They're not building it to bring schools and churches," my father reminded mildly. "They're building it to make it pay. They want to lay down eight hundred miles west and south in the territory. It's to cost eighteen thousand dollars a mile or more. That's fourteen million dollars." He ran his hand over his unruly black beard. "Fourteen million dollars when we already have trails that cost nothing and freighters who've built up their trains to more than five thousand steers and mules."

"Steers and mules!" My mother's eyes were blazing. "Have steers and mules ever civilized this country? How many shooting scrapes does the Capitan *Enterprise* print every week? Murders, they should be called—cold-blooded murders! And that doesn't count the lynchings and men who disappear and the women and children scalped by your friends the Apaches! Is it any wonder that good people refuse to come to this barbarous country?"

My father looked very humble.

"Aren't you confusing it, Nettie, with farming country like Kansas?" he asked. "That's a new country. This is old. White people have been here for hundreds of years, but they never got very far with farming. I've heard you say yourself it's only a desert. But this young promoter, Rutherford"—I saw Juliana's eyelashes quiver—"wants to spend fourteen million dollars to give the desert a railroad. He tells our towns to go in debt with bonds and buy railroad stock with the money. He tells them the railroad will some day be one of the biggest in the country."

I saw that my mother was staggered despite herself by the unanswerable facts and figures. She leaned forward appealingly.

"When one of your Mexican herders' relatives gets into trouble, Frank, you always feel sorry and help him out. Can't you feel sorry for an American who isn't much more than a boy, who works for the railroad company and believes what the higher officials tell him?"

"No," my father said slowly, and it was the first hardness I had heard in his voice since he had entered the room. I saw that he had straightened. "I have sympathy, Nettie, for a man who knows he is gambling and loses, and for a man who knows he may get hung for stealing a horse and steals it. But I have none for anyone who throws away other people's hard-earned money, who's gullible enough to swallow a wild dream like a fourteen-million-dollar railroad on the desert." He looked straight at my mother and went on, drawing in his bearded lips with great force: "Such a waster will never become a member of my house—not while I'm alive!"

There were streaks of chalk in my mother's cheeks, but what is hard to forget is Juliana. Quiet, the locket still moving gently on her dove-colored bodice, she sat on her chair, and her face was no paler than when she had come in. But the eyes that stared at my father were the eyes of a dead person. I was aware of my mother laying her ringed fingers, as if for divine strength, on the gilded covers of the thick family Bible that lay on the table beside her.

"God will punish you, Frank Gant!" she said.

Now that he had taken his position, my father had become his old self again, firm, robust, Atlantean, almost like a Nubian lion in his black beard and broadcloth, standing there with such living power that I felt that words, shafts, bullets and even the hand of God must glance off from him.

"Perhaps Julie feels badly now," he went on confidently, "but she'll get over it till I get back. My early clip's started to move east, and I'm leaving for St. Louis in the morning to sell it."

The plains had deepened in grass to my pony's knees before my father returned. He always remembered me from the St. Louis shops, with something not easily obtainable in his store—a boy's light rifle or silver spurs. Usually his gifts for Juliana were slighter—a sterling napkin-ring engraved with her name, a golden-leather album with the photographs of President and Mrs. Hayes in front, and once a mahogany lap secretary. I know that secretly he was very fond of her, but she was only a girl, an heir who would never carry on his name or smoke heavy cigars while making contracts with Kansas City jobbers or colonels of the quartermaster's department, or drive a buggy over a region half as large as New England, overseeing the lambing of a vast number of ewes and sleeping among the herders in all kinds of spring weather.

But no one could predict my father. When, hale, lusty, and radiating vitality, he left the mansion for the store, after greeting us on his return far ahead of his mule train, Trinidad brought in two canvas valises from the boot of a new buggy.

There were, I remember, taffetas and alpacas for my mother, but most of it, I glimpsed at once, was for Juliana. My mother held them up to her, one after the other, but all I can recall are a blue velvet riding-dress with an extraordinarily long skirt and a black, lathlike sheath dress, a style none of us had ever seen before, and in which, my mother promptly declared, no self-respecting girl would show her figure or could walk across the room if she did.

When I ran to the store with my new, silver-mounted bridle that was on the bottom of the second valise, my father glanced at me sharply.

"What did Juliana say?" he questioned. "Did she try on the dresses?"

I felt a faint chill up my spine, but one look at his eyes convinced me that I must tell the truth. No one today has eyes like his, blue-green in his black beard, leaping at times with a gusto that would stop at nothing, burning again with a deadly green flame and as quickly freezing to blue ice.

"I don't reckon she was feeling good, papa," I stammered. "She just went to her room and didn't say anything."

Al Sleeper, the head clerk, turned quickly to rearrange the wooden boot-boxes that stood in a pile on the floor, and the faces of the listening men stiffened as if someone had suddenly brushed them all with varnish. But my father's face did not change, neither then nor day after day when I saw him look up with a steeled expression to see what

Juliana was wearing, only to find her monotonously, almost disrespectfully, in the dove-colored gray.

Something had happened to Juliana. There was a spring in a *cañada* of the San Blas plain that the Mexicans called El Olvidado. The grass was never so green as there, with a fringe of tules and red-winged blackbirds and the living water welling up cool and clear. My pony and I had often drunk there. But the last year something strange had come to the place. The tules were still there and the red-winged blackbirds, and the grass still looked green, but there was no water to drink.

It was like that with Juliana. She had the same clear skin and straight white path running back along the center of her smoothly parted, dark hair, and the heart-shaped locket still stirred to her breathing, but something clear and living had vanished. Her custom-made sidesaddle gathered gritty plains dust in the harness room, and her cream-colored buckskin mare grew wild on the range. Most of the time she spent quietly in her room, and when I came in, she would be sitting on the edge of her bed, a two-months-old copy of the New York *Ledger* or *Saturday Night* in her fingers, but her eyes would be gazing over the top of the pages and out of the deep window to the plain that already, in August, was a gray, imprisoning sea.

People in the territory were not different from people anywhere else, and I knew they were talking. Whenever Juliana was called into my mother's rooms to greet visitors, I saw them exchange guarded glances. And when she crossed to the store to match yarn for my mother's tireless bone needles, seeing almost no one, walking with open eyes like one asleep, customers watched her furtively, and Mexican women murmured sympathetically "*Pobrecita*" after she had gone. My father never murmured in his life, and his full-charged, indomitable figure remained as always, but more than once when my mother was not looking, I watched him glance characteristically at Juliana. And although his bearded face remained adamant, I fancied I could see a kind of Spartan pain afterward in his eyes.

Looking back now, I can understand perfectly, and everything falls into its place like the letters of the alphabet. But I was only a boy on my pony that day in Capitan when lawyer Henry Coddom asked me to come into his house. In the parlor a man was pacing up and down and, even in that dim room so soon after the bright sunlight, I saw at once that it was Vance Rutherford, tall, perhaps a little older, his cheekbones faintly haggard, a fresh desert marigold as always in the buttonhole of his high Eastern coat, and the familiar faraway look in his eyes which to me had never seemed to belong to the long fighting lines of his face.

I stiffened at the sight of him, but Vance Rutherford bowed in his impersonal, gentlemanly manner.

"Good morning, Johnnie," he said gravely, and asked me to sit down on the black horsehair sofa, where, for a time, like a pair of grown men, we spoke formally on trivial subjects, none of which touched the railroad or my family.

"Johnnie," he said quietly after a little, "will you take a letter to your sister and not let anyone else see it?"

He did not try to urge me. I thought of Juliana walking with mute eyes around the mansion, and I told myself that I didn't like to be the one to keep a letter from her.

"I don't care," I said, meaning I would do it, and he brought it out, and without either of us saying another word, I slipped it into a pocket.

The letter burned like a live coal all the way back on the saddle to Gant's, and I felt relieved that my father was in the Merino Valley and that I did not have to smuggle the letter past him like an Indian stalking out of the store with one of our butcher knives under his blanket. All afternoon I

37

watched the men shovel the new crop of barley and corn into the dusty warehouse bins, and when I put my saddle and bridle away in the harness room in the last golden, stabbing rays of the sun, I found, with surprise, that Juliana's sidesaddle was missing. She did not come to the table for supper, and when I heard the long, doleful bugle of a prairie wolf after nightfall, I went to my mother.

"It's all right, John," she said, and I think she knew about the letter then. "Someone will see Juliana home or she'll stay all night at the Hudspeths'."

It was during the heavy hours of the night that I was awakened by the feel of a kiss on my cheek. I twisted my head on the bolster, and there was Juliana with a lighted candlestick in her hand. She didn't say a word, just stood there looking down at me, and there was in her face a shining something I had never seen before. It wasn't altogether real—the late hour, her illuminated figure against the blackness of the huge room, the strange luminosity in her eyes, and her appearance in the stunning blue velvet riding-dress my father had brought her. I had the singular impression that it was a dream, but when I reached out to see if I could touch her, she squeezed my fingers and I found her hand substantial and throbbing with warmth.

I thought it strange that she was not at breakfast, and when I looked into her room, the smoothness of the bright, quilted counterpane told me that her bed had not been slept in. Lupita and Piedad, two of the Mexican servants, professed to know nothing about it, but I knew, by the impassive restraint in which they moved away, that a feeling of excitement pervaded the house. And as I passed my mother's open door, I saw her wiping her eyes.

That afternoon my father drove home in time for supper. His beard was roan from the trail, and his eyes glinted through it like pieces of turquoise in the dust. As a rule, my mother took her meals in her rooms, where she ate in lone state from a massive silver tray covered with hammered dots. And I felt the keen import tonight when her full taffeta skirts came rustling to the dining room.

I think my father sensed it too. Twice I saw him glance deliberately at the empty chair standing with such silent power at the table. And before he spoke, his bearded lips tightened.

"Where's Juliana?" he asked, and the brown face of Lupita, the table girl, grew thin with emotion. But my mother's eyes burned with a triumphant light across the table.

"She's gone!" she told him, as if she had waited long for this moment. "She was married to Vance Rutherford at the Coddoms' last evening. They're halfway to Kansas by now."

I did not dare look at my father. Sitting there with my dark antelope steak smoking on the plate before me, I suddenly knew why Juliana had come in during the night to kiss me. And for a long, vivid moment I could see her in her blue velvet and Vance Rutherford with a fresh desert marigold in his buttonhole sitting close together in the bridal coach as they swept northeast across the territory, followed by a golden whirlwind of earthy cloud. And now, hours after they had left, it was as if I could still see their dust lying over the plain in the calm October sunlight like a long, motionless finger pointing out to my father the direction they had gone.

Every second I expected to hear him push back his chair and call for Trinidad to hitch Prince and Custer, his fastest buggy team. When at last I looked up, he had regained his indomitable control. But his face was like the faint grayness of winter snow through the heavy growth of black spruce on lone, powerful Mount Jeddo.

He did not speak during the rest of the supper. Lupita tiptoed around the table. The meal lasted interminably. For all of my father's lack of hunger, he did not allow himself to eat a mouthful less than customary. When he rose to go to the store, which always stayed open till ten o'clock, he must have been aware that every clerk and customer would by this time probably know. His beard and shoulders up, the deep smoldering fire in his eyes warning everyone he met, he walked steadily across the trail in the dusk.

Juliana wrote to my mother, letters filled with bright pictures of her new life. She and Vance lived in a beautiful brick house with a marble doorstep in Kansas City. She had bought a stunning maroon cheviot suit with pearl buttons and a bonnet with plumes to match. Every Sunday morning she and Vance attended church, and already at weekday breakfast she knew the day's news of the world. Her letters closed: "Give my dearest love to papa and Johnnie. Your affectionate daughter, Juliana." But if my mother ever ventured to give it, I never heard her.

All winter I did not mention her name to my father and never heard him speak it. I doubted if he ever would. When, sometimes, I would see him walking silently and rigidly about the place, it was as if he were trying by sheer force of will to erase her ghostlike presence from our hall and rooms, from the aisles of the store, and even from the territory. By the following spring it almost seemed as if she might never have been there. But once my mother read aloud from the *Enterprise* that Mr. and Mrs. Henry Coddom had been to Kansas City, and when she came to the words "they called on Mrs. Vance Rutherford, the former Juliana Gant," something wrenched open in my mind and Juliana was back in the mansion with us as real as she had ever been in the flesh.

It was only in this way she came that windy day in April when the dust was flying in yellow sheets across the plain. A private coach had stopped to buy grain for the horses at our feed corral. Someone walked into the mansion courtyard, and old Piedad came hurrying back through the hall with a kind of consternation on her wrinkled face. Rather curiously, I went to the door and for a moment had the feeling that Juliana had come. It was Vance Rutherford, a little heavier and more mature, his face solid and squarer, with a reddish mustache and a marigold as always in his buttonhole.

I stood uncomfortably in the doorway, not knowing quite what to do or say, but Piedad had gone on to my mother's rooms, and now my mother came with loud sibilations of taffeta skirts, seized both of Vance Rutherford's hands in hers, kissed him as if he were my brother, and poured out a dozen questions about Juliana.

"Juliana's fine," he said. "She wanted to come along, but I'm on business." His face sobered. "I've got to see Mr. Gant in the store and then hurry back, but I promised to see you first, so I could tell her how you all looked."

At the mention of my father, the bright, birdlike glint came into my mother's eyes. I saw that she itched to know the cause of his visit, but he did not offer to tell her, and when he left for the store, she feverishly insisted that I go along, as if my companionship might in some mysterious brotherly manner ingratiate him into my father's good graces.

It was the last place in the world that I wanted to be at the moment, and I kicked grimly at every bone and horn I met in the dust to the wide store steps. Through the open door I could see my father standing in a circle of respectfully listening men, his back and clasped hands to the cold, fat-bellied, unblackened stove. Then I stepped discreetly aside to let Vance Rutherford enter first.

It could not have been possible for more than a few of our customers to know Vance Rutherford by sight; yet when

41

he stepped past the pile of carriage blankets at the door, something was in the air of the big store room that wasn't there before. Ike Roehl, halfway up a stepladder, soundlessly dropped an armful of ladies' zephyrs to the counter. Over by the sugar barrels, a clerk and customer stopped talking. In the silence that followed I could hear the windows rattling and the fine sand sifting across the small panes. And suspended on their nails along the ceiling, the rows of wooden buckets kept swinging silently in the draft.

"Could I see you a few minutes in your office, Mr. Gant?" Vance Rutherford asked.

I expected to see rushing into my father's face that volcanic violence from which I had often watched men shrink. Instead, he seemed to be seized by some strange perversity. Not long before, he had come in from overseeing the loading of fleeces on one of his eastbound wagon trains. The rolling brim of his hat was gray with dust. Wisps of wool clung to his broadcloth and buttons. And now he stood with his chin half-sunken on his chest and his eyes half-closed, as if warding off someone he intensely disliked, with a kind of ponderous lethargy.

"Anything you have to say, you can say it here," he rumbled.

Vance Rutherford stood very straight, but I saw him bite his lip.

"I wanted to talk to you in private, sir," he flushed, "so you'd be free to act as you thought best in the matter." He waited a few moments. "If you force me to make it public property, I'll do it." He waited again, and when my father made neither movement nor further expression, his face grew longer and harder, and I saw that it had not lost any of its fighting lines. "The railroad is coming into the territory, sir!" he announced tensely. "We're starting to lay track across the line in May."

Smoke Over the Prairie

None of the listening men moved so much as a finger, but I could feel a wave of something electric sweep over the room. Only my father seemed immune from it. He still stood like a dozing buffalo bull, only partly aware of what might be going on around him.

"You're coming as far as Capitan?" he grunted.

"We'll have trains running into Capitan in a year," Vance Rutherford promised.

My father lifted his massive head, and I saw his deep smoldering eyes.

"You still have railroad stock for sale?"

"We have, Mr. Gant," the younger man said simply. "It takes money to build a railroad."

"I understand," my father rumbled on, "that you figure on spending millions in the territory?"

"Millions!" Vance Rutherford agreed. "But it will all come back to us, once we're in operation." He leaned forward earnestly. "Mr. Gant, you've been a pioneer in this country. You've had to deal with savages and outlaws, but those days are nearly over. The territory is on the threshold of prosperity. A flood of people are coming with the railroad. Schools and churches will spring up everywhere. It's going to be an empire, the Southwestern empire, sir. I can see the railroad a few years from now hauling train after train of passengers and rich freight all the vast distance from the Mississippi to the Pacific!"

I was fascinated by his eloquence. There was something magically convincing in his voice and enthusiasm, and for the moment I could actually see a railroad train sweeping triumphantly across our San Blas plain, and the Indians and Mexicans fleeing from it in terror. And, looking into the staring eyes of grizzled old teamsters, I believed they could see it too.

Vance Rutherford seemed to feel his power. He went

43

on appealingly: "Mr. Gant, you're one of the biggest freighters in the country. You know your business, and if you do,
you must know that the day of mule and bull trains is past.
You've seen what happened along the Santa Fe trail in
Kansas. You know what will happen to the wagon business
in this territory as soon as we have trains running into
Capitan. Don't you agree, sir, that it's good business for a
freighter to sell his wagons and mules while there's a demand and put his money into the railroad?"

I heard a sound like a deep mutter that could be no
longer withheld, and before I looked I knew that my father
had thrown up his massive head and was standing there,
rude and immovable, his shaggy beard throwing off defiance, and green fire like the dog star in his eyes.

"No!" he bellowed, and I heard the tinware on the
shelves murmur his decree after him. "My only interest in
your stock, young man, was to find out whether I could
trust you and your fourteen-million-dollar-railroad officials
to horse feed when they came through!"

I saw Al Sleeper open his mouth in a soundless laugh
and a rancher from the Tres Ritos bring one hand down
silently on his denim thigh. The spell of the railroad was
irreparably broken. Customers and loafers nudged one another, and Vance Rutherford looked as if he had been
struck across the face. His temples twitched, but he stood
his ground.

"I think, Mr. Gant," he said, with a great effort at
dignity, "if the railroad ever asks it, your feed corral would
be justified in extending credit."

I expected him to go, but for a long moment the two
men continued to face each other—both iron-willed and
unyielding; one, young in years, gentlemanly, with a flower
in his buttonhole; the other, older, powerful, with streaks
of wool and dust on his clothing; one of the new age, one

of the old. Then the younger man turned silently and went out.

News of the coming of the railroad spread like a gold strike through the territory. Stories reached the store by stage and wagon train, by buckboard and carriage. The railroad was awarding contracts for grading, ties, bridge timbers and telegraph poles. The railroad contractors were buying herds of horses and mules. The railroad was blasting tunnels through the San Dimas Mountains. The railroad was crossing the mountains on the old wagon trail. All summer and fall the railroad expected to lay from one to two miles of track a day.

By Christmas the byword among the teamsters returning from the iron rails was: "Look out for the locomotive!" They reported the sleepy old Mexican village of La Luz booming since the railroad had arrived. The Capitan *Enterprise* announced with pride that Baldwin's were building a new, huge, eighty-ton locomotive for use in the territory and that it would be "in charge of men fully competent to handle the monster." And it added that Vance Rutherford, engineer for the railroad, had promised lawyer Henry Coddom that he was pushing construction with every resource at his command and that trains would be running into Capitan by the Fourth of July.

In the very next issue of the *Enterprise*, Capitan stores advertised in tall type that no new merchandise would come from the East until it arrived more cheaply and safely by steam train. My mother had always abhorred the trail, its clouds of dust, the shouts and curses of its drivers, the crack of whips and report of linchpins, and the snail-like drag of long files of chained steers. Ever since I could remember, she had shut it out with heavy brown hangings. But now she began to draw them back and sit at her knitting where she could see, at last, traffic slowly but steadily fading like late afternoon on the old trail. It seemed to give her a satisfaction as if the railroad were just over the rise, ruthlessly pushing the creaking freight wagons out of the way.

I knew that every vanished wagon sheet and silent wheel was a secret growing cancer in the heart of my father. He never alluded to it, but when I rode along in his buggy to Capitan, I could see the steely glitter in his eyes at sight of the copper ingots, which his trains formerly freighted to Kansas, piling up in great mounds at the proposed site of the new depot. And his eyes looked straight ahead when we passed teams unloading wool and hides into adobe warehouses that had sprung up like molehills where Henry Coddom had sold the railroad a tract of land for the new Capitan town site and which, already, people were calling Newtown.

There was actually no more railroad to be seen in Capitan than out on the sand hills, but every day now rigs began passing our store on their way to Capitan to trade. Cowboys nightly celebrated the railroad by shooting up the town. There was talk of the *Enterprise* becoming a daily after the telegraph had arrived. I saw where Strome Brothers had torn down their old wooden hitching-rack and set up individual posts with citified snap chains. And the *Enterprise* boasted that there wasn't a vacant house in the town.

Up to this time I had never seen a railroad in my young life, and it seemed that our store and trail were being blighted by some mysterious and invisible weapon in Vance Rutherford's hand. This morning I noticed my father throw up his head to gaze at the northeast. When I looked, there it hung like a black dust cloud over the green of the prairie, the railroad at last. And as my father stared at the smoke funneling up persistently on the distant horizon, I saw the same wild defiance come into his bearded face as had that day at his sheep camp along the Rio Cedro when we had watched a Comanche or Kiowa smoke signal from the hills.

Every morning after this the smoke was there, and I came to think of it as the powerful black breath of Vance Rutherford, moving steadily, silently, inexorably southwest toward Capitan. Now it passed the red mesa, and now for a few days it changed rugged Mount Jeddo into an active volcano. And one day when it had reached some miles abreast of us, I could not resist galloping my pony secretly across the plain to a grassy swell from which I could see a whole bank being sliced away like cake. The prairie there seemed to boil with men and teams, with wagons, plows and drags. The air was filled with the flash of moving picks and shovels and the ring of iron hammers. And creeping back and forward in the background, hissing, sometimes out-shrieking any mountain lion, glided one of Vance Rutherford's tamed iron monsters.

I was only a boy, but I could tell, as I rode thoughtfully homeward, that in this thing my mother called civilization there was no quarter, no compromise, no pity. It was not like your grazing pony that, after tiring you for an hour, would let you catch it, or like a wagon train that welcomed you with a blanket, food and the red warmth of a campfire. This was something of another kidney, of another and newer age.

After that initial challenging scrutiny, I never saw my father acknowledge the black smoke's presence. When he entered the store, the subject changed. Only once I heard him refer again to the railroad. A passenger on the halted stage boasted that a Mississippi–Pacific train had done twenty-five miles an hour crossing the plains. My father turned with heavy deliberation and stared him into confusion.

"Sir, I can do as much with one of my Kentucky buggy

teams!" he scorned. "And if the trail is uphill, I have gold to wager that I can soundly whip your train!"

But some hours after the stage had gone, I saw him silent and solitary behind our warehouse, pacing measuredly around what none of us had ever seen before—a corral of his stilled freight wagons. Mute, deserted, and depressing they stood there, an unforgettable reminder of what had been. And late that evening when my mother sent me to take the St. Louis paper back to his office, I don't think he knew I was there, for I heard from his bedroom deep incredible sounds, like a man praying, which instantly riveted me to the floor. I couldn't understand a word he said, but the shock of hearing my strong father give way like that in secret shook me to my foundations.

Next morning at breakfast he was stanch and powerful as always, and I told myself that I must have been mistaken. And that afternoon I felt sure of it. I was counting twenty-, ten- and five-dollar gold pieces, silver dollars, halves and quarters—there was nothing smaller—on his battered desk in the mansion office when through the window I saw lawyer Henry Coddom climb determinedly out of his phaeton in the courtyard. The two men had not met since Juliana had been married in the Coddom parlor, and now, with Henry Coddom appointed attorney for the railroad in the territory, I could feel the clouds gather and thicken. When Piedad brought the visitor to the office door, he asked to speak with my father in private, and I was sent away.

Twenty minutes later Henry Coddom came out like a cuffed schoolboy, hat in his hand, his face crimson. And when my father stepped into the hall to order me back to my counting, there were still pitchforks in his eyes and I had never seen him more absolute and unconquerable. Then he became aware of my mother standing in the doorway to her rooms, color in her quilted cheeks and a newspaper in her hand.

"Nettie"—he inclined his head.

"Frank!" she begged him. "You didn't throw away your invitation?"

"Invitation?" His uncompromising eyes bored her.

"It's in the *Enterprise!*" my mother went on feverishly. "They're running the first train into Capitan the Fourth of July. The whole territory's going to celebrate. They expect crowds from every county. The governor and judges and politicos and all the big men of the territory will get on the train at La Luz and ride into Capitan. The governor of Kansas and his wife will be on the train and a Kansas band. They've telegraphed an invitation to President Hayes."

Granite had come into my father's face.

"I got no invitation," he answered harshly. "Henry Coddom came to tell me the railroad wants to build to California." His eyes blazed. "They want eighty miles of my land. They want to build through the Canyon Bonito. They want to blacken my grass, plow trains through my sheep, dump squatters along the Bonito all the way from Big Flat to Gant's Valley."

I am not sure that my mother heard him.

"Frank," she went on desperately, "it's to be the biggest thing that ever happened in the territory. The railroad's giving a banquet at the Wooton House. There'll be dancing till morning. And all the railroad officials and their wives will be there!"

It was almost as if my mother had mentioned Vance Rutherford and Juliana by name. With a titanic effort to control himself, my father turned without a word into the mansion office. And all the time my fingers kept building up fat piles of white and yellow coins, I could feel the raw emotion working in him. And from the next issue of the *Enterprise* we found that the railroad company was daring to drag him soon, like some petty thief or cattle rustler, into court in Bonito County, half of whose vast spaces he owned, to show why eighty miles of his choicest river pastureland should not be condemned for the railroad right-of-way.

For days afterward he remained around home, silent and implacable, waiting for the case to be called. And when I saw the dull fire leaping in his eyes, I knew he was forging the bolts of lightning he would let loose in that small adobe courtroom at Bonito. Of course Mr. Stryker, his lawyer, would be with him, but it was my father who would dominate the court.

"No judge in this territory," Al Sleeper declared, "can look Frank Gant in the eye and turn over his land to Henry Coddom and a Kansas railroad."

For weeks my father waited while the railroad pushed its mailed arm into Capitan, while June grew closer to July, and Juliana's cream-colored mare had a second colt that Juliana had never seen. And all the time I could see in my mother's eyes the hope that the case had not yet been called in Judge Tatum's court at Bonito, because he and Vance Rutherford expected to come to my father privately and settle the differences out of court in time to get him to the celebration. I knew that if anybody could reason with my father it was Judge Tatum, whom I had often seen slouched in the mansion office, an extraordinarily long figure with a face like a sorrel horse, his long legs up on the battered desk, a thick tumbler and a jug of my father's whisky beside him, and my father laughing indulgently through his beard at what the judge was saying.

Then all hope of my father going to the celebration faded from my mother's eyes. One of his old herders, Gil Jaramillo, arrived in the mansion courtyard on a spent horse. Tall and cadaverous, his eyes rolling with the mad light of so many men who spend their lives with the sheep, he called out, "*Amo!*" with excitement as soon as he was at the door. And when my father had come into the hall, he stammered out in Spanish that the Cross V's, whose cattle ranch adjoined my father's Rio Cedro pastures, were warring on his sheep, driving some of them into the river, scattering the rest to be preyed upon by coyotes and wolves, and badly beating up the *caporal* and herders.

I expected to see the anger flame on my father's face. Instead it grew calmer than for weeks, as if news of violence and bloodshed was almost a welcome relief from this petty waiting for a summons to court. Within the hour he drove off for the Rio Cedro, sitting in his buggy like a king, Trinidad brown and solid beside him, and a change of horses galloping through the dust behind. And long after he had gone I could see him in my mind, whipping his team across a region half as wide as France, the goats leaping with flying beards from in front of the horses, the cedar branches whipping the buggy from both sides of the narrow trail, himself staying the night in some humble *placita* and, if there was a bed in the village, sleeping in it, and finally matching his strength against his enemies, who had always been putty in his hands.

I was glad he had gone that evening when the deputy from Bonito County arrived apologetically with the summons. But the gray glance of Al Sleeper held a queer light, and under his mustache, jutting out from his face like the waterfall of a roily mountain stream, his mouth looked forbidding. He spoke to my mother and early next morning sent the summons with a Mexican rider after my father, but I knew it was like a desert finch trying to catch an eagle.

The mansion seemed like a convent with my father gone. Our native villagers kept asking if we were not to ride with the governor on the bunting-trimmed train. I told them we didn't like crowds, that we had plenty of bunting in the mansion and that we intended to wait until there was room in Capitan to breathe. They nodded solemnly, polite Mexicans that they were, but they knew as well as I why we weren't going.

And now from morning till night the migration toward Capitan began passing our door—American ranchers and miners on the saddle, in buggy and buckboard; officers' families from Fort Gates in Army ambulances with the side curtains rolled up for air; but mostly natives who had never seen the iron horse; Mexican families in heavy wagons, in a few private carriages, and on endless saddles; Ute Indians decked with bright ribbons, their bony ponies packed for trade; and aloof Navajos in red calicoes and blue velvets and clinking silver.

By noon of the Fourth all had passed. The last trip the stage would ever make by our door took place about one, the westbound coach crowded with passengers. It threw off our leather bag of mail, but failed to stop. And after it had gone and the trail lay quiet again, I suddenly realized that it looked different from what I had ever seen it, old, tired, abandoned, almost like the ruins of an ancient *camino* winding desolately over the plain.

About two o'clock I glimpsed a distant smudge of dust to the northeast, a smudge that swirled rapidly nearer, and finally I could make out our bay team plunging wearily toward home, my father driving and Trinidad still beside him, but only one horse galloping behind. My father swerved the foaming, bulging-eyed team into the mansion courtyard. As I slipped back into the hall, he said something to Trinidad, who at once drove away. Then I saw through my mother's doorway that she had stiffened in her chair and bent her face defensively over her knitting.

My father scarcely tossed a glance at me as he came in, haggard and grim, his hat, beard and broadcloth layered with dust. He halted in the center of the hall, from where his eyes could flash turbulently into my mother's room.

"Was Stryker here to see me?"

My mother's rigid needles kept moving.

Smoke Over the Prairie

"Yesterday, Frank," she answered.

"Well?" he breathed heavily.

"Judge Tatum appointed commissioners to condemn the land." My mother's lips were tight bands. "He told Mr. Stryker that no individual could stand in the way of progress and the railroad."

My father hadn't moved. My mother tried to leave the subject: "Did you settle the trouble with the Cross V's?"

"There was," my father answered harshly, "no trouble to settle."

"What do you mean?" For the first time she looked up at him.

"I mean," my father said, and now that he had started, the words poured out in a wild torrent, "that progress isn't above using the tricks of a blackleg gambler!" The green lightning had leaped from his eyes and at each successive sentence the bolt seemed to hurl itself again, as I had often watched it in a distant cloud, traversing over and over the same forked path. "There wasn't any sheep war. Nobody had beaten a herder. I didn't find a ewe touched. Somebody paid Gil Jaramillo to come here. They bribed him to lie to me. They had me drive hundreds of miles in a buggy and kill one of my best horses to keep me away from Judge Tatum's court!" Then he turned and went into his office.

I thought I could hear him moving about in his bedroom. There was a purr of wheels in the courtyard, and through the pane at the side of the door I saw Trinidad drive up in the red-wheeled buggy without a top.

My father came out almost immediately. He had changed his clothes, but the dust still clung to his beard and eyebrows. In his hand was the black-snake whip with which he had once whipped a herder for the arch crime of deserting his sheep, and I saw that the lash was still caked with dried particles of red.

53

"Frank!" my mother cried. She had run to her doorway. "Where are you going?"

He paid her utterly no attention. I don't think he knew she was there.

"Frank!" she screamed after him. "Whoever bribed Gil Jaramillo, it wasn't Vance Rutherford or the railroad! They wouldn't stoop to a thing like that!"

He went on out of the door. Never had I seen my mother move so rapidly. Her full skirts seemed to whisper in terror as they glided over the floor. Her hands seized my shoulder.

"Get him to take you with him!" she begged me. "He never does those violent things when you're along!" She pushed me out of the doorway and I saw the sun glinting on the sleek flanks of the dancing Kentucky team.

I ran to the right side, where the springs had already deeply settled.

"I want to go along, papa!" I shouted at him.

He looked down at me.

"You're sure you want to go along?" he asked, and at his mad eyes a chill ran down my spine, but I nodded. He told the impassive Trinidad to step out, and I climbed in beside him. Prince and Custer were crazy to be off. They had not been driven for days. One hand of my father pulled them back, rearing.

"Easy, boys," he said through his teeth and beard. "We'll have plenty time when we get there."

Crouching on the cushion, I told myself I couldn't see how trouble could happen on a day like this. The sky was a blue bowl and I could smell the freshness of last night's shower in the bunch grass all around us. Horned larks flushed in front of the horses. A road runner clowned at us, his crest and long tail rising and falling comically. But I did not laugh. Ahead, like a bed of mushrooms sprung up on the prairie, I could see the buildings of Capitan.

54

Smoke Over the Prairie

Halfway across the prairie something ran shining through the grass—the twin iron bands of the railroad. From here to Capitan they had built straight as an arrow, close beside the trail, as if to ridicule the earthy ruts, crude windings and arroyo dips of the sprawling old overland route. Here the railroad cut insolently over the trail, and the light buggy pitched on the rough planks of the crossing, but my father gave no sign that the railroad was there—not even when a wailing cry drifted over the prairie behind us and I knew without turning my head that the horizon must be stormy with smoke.

Within a mile or two the rails only a few yards from the trail were crackling. Our Kentucky buggy horses had grown uneasy and were trying to throw frightened looks over their shoulders, but my father held their heads with an iron hand. Twisting in my seat, I could see the afternoon sun sparkling on something that moved behind us, pursuing us, not galloping up and down like a buffalo, but gliding through the grass like a snake. The bulging smokestack was as high as the neck of a camel, the boiler as big as the belly of a horse, and below it a cowcatcher, long and pointed like Judge Tatum's nose, ran on its own pony wheels. A man rode in the cab that was as high off the ground as a buggy, and behind him streamed the coaches of the territory's celebration train.

I could hear a brass band in the cars now. It was playing "Dixie." Everything on the train was gaiety as it pulled beside us. Red, white and blue bunting fluttered from headlight, smokestack and whistle. The bell rang triumphantly. The small pony wheels spun. The black-and-gold driving shafts shot backward and forward. Faces pressed at the small, square windows, and on the open platforms of the short, boxlike coaches a few male passengers stood holding to iron railings and brake wheels. But for all the attention my father gave it, the train might not have been there.

So far the railroad and train had been slightly downhill. Now the train reached the foot of the steady prairie grade up to Capitan. The engine began to puff valiantly, and a cloud of cinders came flying back into our faces. Suddenly I realized that, although my father still sat like a bearded statue beside me, his thewlike fingers had let out some slack on the lines, and the long-denied horses were leaping.

I told myself it couldn't be a race, because my father wasn't racing. He just sat there deaf and unapproachable, but now I know that of all the matches between horseflesh and the iron horse that were to follow on the same rude course, this was the most intense and deadly in earnest. Heads began to appear out of the open car windows. Passengers waved, jeered and challenged. But the train no longer was moving faster than the buggy.

Suddenly something inside of me seemed to stand still. Peering round my father, I had caught a glimpse of a face at a car window. It was more of a lady's face than I had remembered, but the eyes under the nodding plumes were unchanged. They were fixed on my father with a look that I shall never forget, almost the look they had given him that day she had tiptoed into my mother's room two years before, a straining look of appeal that might almost have been at God. Only a matter of thirty or forty feet separated her from my father, but it might as well have been the width of Kansas. He did not turn. The horses raced on, and when I looked again, all I could see in the glass was the blurred reflection of prairie sky, and the face of Juliana had gone.

I had to keep bracing myself on the rocking cushion. The train beside us rode smoothly enough, almost contemptuously, over its new roadbed, but the buggy plunged from rut to pitch hole, and yet, window by window and now coach by coach, the buggy was gaining. Directly ahead I could make out a dense frieze of men's hats and ladies' parasols around the new depot. Nearer, on both sides of the railroad, the green plain blossomed with visiting tents and camp wagons. And now the trail just in front of us began to teem with American, Mexican and Indian spectators, who fell back whooping and shouting as we tore by.

I can still see Prince and Custer running, their heads outstretched, their manes wildly flinging, and at every jump the fine muscles on their hips appearing and disappearing like so many fingered hands. With both horses bent into shying half arcs, we breasted the laboring engine, passed it, left its bright flutter of bunting definitely behind us. And I told myself exultantly that my father had whipped the celebration train, humbled the railroad in front of half the territory. Then I saw ahead where the trail swerved sharply, and remembered that we had another crossing in store.

There was no necessity for my father to take it. He might have turned off the trail on the unfenced prairie. But my father never turned off the trail for anything, God or the devil, cruelty or mercy; so long as it lay squarely in his path, he knew no other justice. Leaning far to the side for the curve, he snatched the whip from its socket and the buggy reeled on two wheels for the crossing.

Through the din of the train I could hear the band playing magnificently. It sounded like "Columbia, the Gem of the Ocean." High above it shrieked the voice of the engine whistling down brakes for the station. It seemed far enough away when it started, grew steadily louder, louder, till the sound seemed to split my ear. I saw my father drop the reins and felt him swing me up in his arms. There was a sound like chair legs crashing, and the blurred earth, engine, and the white faces of the engineer and frontier crowd turned over like the markings on a grindstone.

It wasn't exactly a pain in my back. I felt benumbed,

as if an arrow pinned me down. My eyes seemed to be ground shut with dust and sand, and when I forced them open, I could see nothing but the dude hats of men who had come from the train and the gaily trimmed bonnets of the ladies all swimming around me in a kind of leisurely whirlwind.

Only one of the bonnets looked familiar. It was very near, fashioned with drooping plumes, and I knew that somewhere I had seen it before.

A portly man in a long coat with a velvet collar thrust a flask to my lips. I sputtered and strangled, but when I could breathe again, I felt better.

"Where's my father?" I asked them.

They all just stood there looking at me. I twisted my head and saw Vance Rutherford. He was close to me, a flower in his buttonhole, comforting Juliana, who was bitterly crying. When I closed my eyes I could still see my father sitting in the buggy beside me, aloof, powerful, absolute, his black beard turned stubbornly in the wind, the reins in his thewlike fingers. All these men from the train looked white and soft in comparison. They couldn't, I told myself, whip the bloody back of a herder who had broken the trust to his sheep. I wanted my father. One bark from his bearded lips, and most of this crowd would scurry like prairie dogs.

"Where'd he go?" I cried, and struggled to sit up. Vance Rutherford and the portly man helped me. The crowd fell back slightly. All I could see between tailored trousers and gaily flounced dresses were the iron bands of the railroad running triumphantly westward and glinting like mottled silver in the sun.

 # The Flood

IT'S GONE NOW, receded and dried up, so that amid all the peace and plenty long since dwelling on its shores, you can hardly find a living trace of it, save in the history books, the war colleges and in the Gettysburg words of Abraham Lincoln. And yet once not so long ago that flood flowed like a tide of blood two thousand miles across the country, dyeing rivers, engulfing farms, climbing mountains and penetrating the quiet valleys between. It even reached its long red arm across the endless plains of Texas, and if you look sharp, you may still see it there as it was then, sweeping from saddle to saddle, and from remote ranch house to ranch house, pulling men from horses and lonely pallets and starting them toward the distant front.

That's what it had done to Coe Elliot. Rigged out in his newly sewn suit of gray, he stood in this Texas town room with the alien young woman at his side, and in front of them the gaunt circuit preacher with a fierce look on his face and the open Book in his veined hands.

The preacher's voice grew sterner. "Coe Ellyit, do you take this lady, Bethiah Todd, as your lawful wife till death do you part?"

Now he was in for it, Coe thought. He would ride a thousand miles to get at those fool Yankees who reckoned they could tell the South what it had to do. He would leave his herd of longhorns scattered over the Nogal plain and his half dugout in the little Mexican settlement on the flat between the river and his spring. But riding the ninety miles into town yesterday and day before, he had wished he had a woman to leave behind, somebody to think of him when he was away and to come back to when the war was over. And that was a funny thing to wish, for white women were scarce as prairie chickens' teeth out in this new Texas country.

"I do," he said, and anybody, knowing Coe or not, could have told from that hard, tanned face that he would keep his word.

The gaunt Texas preacher turned to the girl. The blight of his eyes was on her. You could see he had nothing for this marriage. He might have Christian pity on her for her plight, but that was as far as his religion bade him go.

"Bethiah Todd, do you take this man, Coe Ellyit, as your lawful husband till death do you part?"

That's the way she had looked, Coe told himself, when they had brought her to town with the oxen and wagon after the Comanches had ambushed her father. They had got him at the river, with a cedar pail in one hand and a tin cup in the other, and they had nigh split his head open with their scalping. He was a plowman from Kentucky, out here for free land. He was big and shut-mouthed and dark, they said, and his daughter was little and slight and white as milk in her red dress against those jetty-black oxen. But now she was shut-mouthed too. Her little wisp of a face was set and her lips tight at what had overtaken her. Her eyes were dead and hopeless.

She had no place to go, Coe Elliot had thought with pity when he saw her, and he had spoken before he had weighed it.

"I can give you a home at the ranch," he had told her. "The Mexican women will look after you till I get back from the wars. And if I don't come back, everything I got is yours as my widow."

The Flood

Bitterly she had looked at him then, and in bitter silence consented. And that was the way she answered the preacher now. If she gave him ever a plain word, like "yes" or "sir," it was too low for him to hear it. The preacher looked at her, and finally at Coe, who nodded him to go on.

"Then, with the authority invested in me by the Church of Christ," he declared, "and by the Confederate States of America, I declare you man and wife."

It was mighty quiet in that room now. Nobody made a move to kiss the set little face of the bride.

"All I got to say, Miz Ellyit, you got a mighty fine man," the preacher told her. It was plain that was all he intended to say. He turned away as if in disapproval of the whole business.

"Well, I reckon Miz Ellyit and me'll start for the ranch," the groom took hold of things to say. "We got only five hours till sundown, and steers are mighty slow."

The room kind of froze like the first skim of ice on a slough. The preacher turned around with the half-written marriage paper in his hand. "You're going up there today?"

"I ain't got much time," Coe said pleasantly. "I got to get back or they'll have those Yanks licked before I get a chance at 'em."

Nobody said anything for a little. At the end, the preacher spoke for all. "Couldn't you get there quicker and safer with a team and buggy, Coe?"

"I take it Miz Ellyit wants her fixens along," the bridegroom said. "She has too much in that wagon for a buggy to pack. And anything my wife wants, Reverend, she can have."

"Certainly, Coe, certainly," the preacher boomed in his great voice, but his eyes looked sad and dull. "May you move in the protecting shadow of the Lord's wing all the way."

Coe stole a quiet look at his wife. She stood there like

61

she was deaf to what was being said, and if she wasn't, she was too slight to do anything about it one way or the other. Her eyes never changed when the women wished her a safe journey. And when he hoisted her up to the wagon seat, she felt small and light in his hand as a cured calfskin. But there was a touch of rawhide in her, too, he reckoned, as he tied his mare, Tally, to the strange tailboard.

Far sooner would he have sold the oxen and put horses to the wagon. But he reckoned it might please her to have some creatures she could call by name around the ranch while he was away. Now those ponderous beasts started, hard of horn and soft of eye and muzzle. Some oxen, their owners claimed, were mighty smart walkers, but to Coe the best were like these, slow as land turtles, moaning a little as they let their shoulders into the pull, moving first one foot, then the other. Up the dusty street they went, the wagon lumbering after, the wheels dragging, the spokes turning slow as clock hands. He could see the town folk in their doors and windows, waiting to see the Kentucky plowman's daughter go by, fresh-orphaned and as fresh-married, setting out in a hard and savage world, sitting alone on her high seat while her cowman groom in his spurred boots walked the ground. But Coe didn't mind. He was in no great hurry to get there, for this was his wedding trip, the only time with his bride he'd get. Soon as he landed her at the ranch, he'd have to light out for Houston. Let folks wonder at him if they would. This was his honeymoon. You did queer things when you took a woman. He just hoped no Confederate soldier would happen along to see him plodding on foot in his short-cut cavalry jacket.

A prettier spot for a bride and groom you hardly could find than what he picked for the night. This was no camp along the trail for late travelers to stop and join them. He had turned the oxen off the wheel tracks. Down in a basin behind a long butte, he halted them. The land spread around like a saucer, soft and green with grass, while all the rolling knolls in the distance were stained with violet mist. Quickly he picketed the mare, unyoked the oxen, hobbled them and turned them loose. In a shake he had a fire of low cedar snapping, and the scent of his bacon and coffee stung the crystal-clear evening air. This was nothing. Men always cooked for their womenfolk out on the range. But she never came down from the wagon seat.

"You want to eat up there?" he asked gravely, and passed up the tin plate and cup.

He turned his back with a plainsman's politeness. The tin cup was half-empty when it came down, but the plate had hardly been touched.

"You ought to had eat something," he told her sternly, like a husband should, but she only sat on her wagon seat, staring out over the wild land. He stood there, stiff and clumsy, holding the cup in one hand and plate in the other.

"If you don't want to eat, couldn't you drink the rest of the coffee?"

Her lips moved no more than when the K-town preacher had put the solemn question. But she turned her head. And that was all he got from her—a turn of that slight head for "no," and a nod of that white face for "yes."

"Anything special I can get for you?" he persisted.

A slow turn of the head.

"You feeling all right?"

Not a move from her, neither yes nor no, just a long look at that wide horizon.

"You like this country out here?" he asked hopefully.

She turned on him such a suddenly bitter and terrible face that he felt all his hopes go out of him.

"Well, you better take a little walk before it gets too dark on you," he said kindly. "I'll fix up your bed this end of the wagon. You don't need to be scared of me. I'll have my bed on the ground."

But when he looked again, all the bright mist had gone from the distant hills, and a grayness from a low bank of clouds was creeping over the broad land.

Before closing his eyes, he could smell the rain coming. More rain. It had been raining most of the week. All night he heard the heavy drops pelting wagon top and sideboards. When he looked out along the tongue, he could see heavy lightning playing far ahead. It seemed to hang in that one spot all night. It was too far away to hear the thunder. Just before daylight, he crawled out and rolled up his bed. He didn't want any stray rider to come along and carry the news back to town that the groom had slept under the wagon.

That was a mighty strange day for a bridegroom, he told himself, driving a span of oxen through the rain, walking beside them through mud and puddles, with your bride sitting on the seat above you and never a spoken word between. Sometimes he fell a little behind, so his eyes could study her. What kind of a "creetur" had he married, sitting there with a face white as gyp rock, in a bright red dress above those jetty-black oxen?

What was the name of the place she hailed from, he wondered, and had she brother or sister back there? Why, he didn't even know how old was his bride. Neither would she eat and neither talk. He had heard that women were mighty hard to brand. Now he knew that you might brand them, but they were a long sight harder to break or gentle.

Halfway to noon he remembered the ox hobbles left behind, and he rode back on his mare to find them. The hobbles were gone, but he found where fresh hoofs of two unshod ponies had cut this way and that across the wet camping ground. More than once he took to the mare that day, to sit gravely in the saddle and scan the four horizons.

The Flood

Behind them, K-town had already vanished behind the mesa. Ahead, the nester settlement along the river was still too far away to see. And if any red Comanche pair still followed the wagon, they kept themselves in some arroyo hidden in that blue expanse of sun and rain-streaked plain.

The river had looked much higher when they had come back to it that morning. Last night's rain in the upland country was starting to come down, bringing the Texas earth with it. And it was still raining. All the time they stopped at noon, while the mare cropped and the oxen grazed greedily side by side, as if still in the yoke, looping up the tufts of buffalo grass with their long tongues, the river kept steadily rising. It rained again that night, and next morning, when they started out, the river ran bankfull beside them.

They entered the long *cañada* about noon. For an hour or two they crawled along with higher mesa land on either side and the river winding like a dark snake between. The sun was halfway down the western sky when something made Coe look around. Back where they had passed on dry land only a few minutes before, a thin, dirty stream was spilling over the bank, lapping a little farther as he watched, trickling into the wheel tracks and running down the trail.

"Come on! Buck and Berry! Step up!" he called, swinging his dead father-in-law's whip.

They had only a mile or two to go until the steep escarpment softened and a draw led up to the mesa. But the great plodding beasts never hurried. You could add ton after ton to their load, and they would pull it as long as the wagon would hold it. They would moan softly and lean their stout shoulders into the bows, their tails would twitch and the wheels would be dragged through hell and damnation. But they wouldn't move any faster. Not for flies or whiplash.

The river was still rising. From every upcountry arroyo, wash and fork came the dark tide that could get through the wide *cañada* intake above faster than it could get out of the narrows below. Each time Coe looked around, he could see behind them a chocolate lake spreading, backing up, pushing ever closer to their heels. In the end, the water spread out on the trail ahead, widening and deeping until the team was in it, moving in one continual splash.

Up to now, those stolid, heavy-footed beasts had made little of the water, save to look down at it with their soft, wondering eyes. But once surrounded by it, a change came over them. They had waded many a ford. But they could always see the trail rising up the bank on the other side. Now they moved through an endless lake, and there was no trail to see either here or ahead. Their pace slowed, their great horned heads swung cautiously from side to side, and when the water at last touched their bellies, they stopped dead. No shouting or beating could stir them. There they stood, immovable except for their swaying horns, while the flood slowly rose to engulf them, first their dewlaps, then their gaunt black thighs, and finally the bows of the yoke itself. The water began pouring through the cracks of the wagon. Coe climbed in and piled his wife's goods to the rear, the most valuable on top out of reach of the wetness.

All the while his mare at the tailboard stood covered to her breast. Her eyes were rolling, and now and then she threshed about, backing as far as she could with her neck outstretched, trying to slip her halter. He would have to watch her or she might hang or drown herself.

He looked around for his wife. In all this waste of muddy water, she was drawn up tight as a jackknife. She had clutched her red skirts from below, so they wouldn't be fouled by the water, and now she sat there, small and rigid, her petticoats held between her knees. Her cheeks were like tallow and her small neck mighty hollow and thin. She was sure showing the long strain. With the little she ate and all

66

she went through, it didn't seem like she could go it much longer.

"It ain't safe for you on shore alone, Bethiah," he told her. "But if you get on the mare behind me, I'll ride you up to the Sugareet till I get your wagon there."

She was staring at the oxen. She shook her head. She wouldn't leave her dead pap's jetty-black span, you could tell that. It showed how much he knew about women. A girl could be little and slight as if the wind would blow her away. She could be worn thin to a frazzle, and just when you figured she would go to pieces, she stiffened up and you couldn't break her.

Well, his wife couldn't sit there on the seat all night, he told himself. When he saw a board or plank coming down on this side, he waded the mare out, caught it with his hands or rope and laid it across the front end of the wagon box. By early dusk he had enough, and on this ill-assorted frame he threw down her bed and unrolled it.

"You better get some rest while you can," he told her.

That was a night he wouldn't forget easy, black as pitch, with the rain coming down and the unseen flood all around them. He tried his bed on the narrow seat, but it wouldn't lay right, and he sat there most of the time, listening to the water lapping at the wagon box, feeling with his hand to see how high it had risen. Now and then, some floating object struck the wagon softly and went on. When it was quiet, he could hear the oxen moving their heads in the bows, this way and that, this way and that, all the night through.

When dawn broke, he looked out on a wide and lonely scene. The *cañada* swam from escarpment to escarpment, while out in the center the current rolled with such power that it lifted in riffles above the rest of the flood. It had risen during the night. His mare's neck was nearly covered. She seemed exhausted and half-drowned. Her wild eyes rolled toward either shore, but the oxen stood unchanged. The water flowed over their jetty-black backs. All you could see of them was their rhythmically moving heads sticking out of the water, and that's the way they stood the whole day, without grass or grain, refusing to budge, although from time to time the heavy wagon seemed to lift from the ground and float of itself in the tide.

It rained fitfully most of the time, but the water rose little higher. This was the crest, Coe told himself. An endless assortment of flotsam was coming down now—posts, gates, loose clapboards, drowned cattle and sheep, and pole roofs from adobe walls that had become mud and collapsed. A nester's chicken coop went by in the current, and what looked like a buckboard with the top of its seat bobbing out. He stood out on the tongue and roped a cedar tub, which he hauled into the wagon. It was a very pretty tub, handmade, with alternate red and white cedar staves, but his bride showed it no interest.

At the very top of the flood, a nester's cabin came down. It was made of pine logs that could be cut on the big mesa above Sugareet. He saw it first far up the river. Now it sank, partly covered by water, and now it reared up like it was on springs. He studied hard at it when it came close, but he couldn't make out whose it was, for a cabin sure looked different standing at its homeplace than floating down the river. It went on by, and at the sharp bend swept so wide with the current, it stuck on the shallow wagon side. Coe took his dead pappy-in-law's Kentucky rifle from its buckskin loops on the wagon bows. He'd carry it with him down the river, just in case. He could see back to the wagon all the time.

When his mare waded out, he found it wasn't the whole cabin. It had broken off three or four logs from the ground. The door was still there. The water had swelled the puncheons fast, and that was what had grounded the cabin. He couldn't budge the door, only the little loft shutter. He stood on his saddle and stuck his head in. That was a mighty strange sight in a cabin, to look down from the loft hole into gurgling water, with shelves and stools floating around inside. The flood had eaten out the mud chinking, and the current flowed through the logs like it was cribbing.

A bolster lay across one loft corner, with a pile of clothing beyond, and he reached out a hand to rummage through it. Then he saw all had been laid to keep something from rolling to the loft hole. It was a white baby, a couple of months old.

Must be the Cartwright cabin, he told himself. The babe lay flat on its back, its pinched face toward the roof. Coe studied it a long time before he saw the mite of a mouth twitch.

Now what did he have to come down here for and stick his nose in this cabin, he told himself. He had enough trouble on his hands without a babe. Now he couldn't go off and let it lay! Nor could he ride it on to some woman in Sugareet, for his wife wouldn't go. How he hated to go back and give it to her! She was miffed at him enough, without knowing he had a sick and starved babe to give her, a nameless orphan to tend, one that couldn't lift a finger to wait on itself and would likely die on her hands. Then she'd sull toward him sure. But what could a man do? He could only break it to her easy as he could.

He covered up the bundle so she couldn't see what it was, rode back to shore, up and out to the wagon.

"That was the Cartwright cabin went by, Bethiah," he started in, mighty sober. "Jim's off to the Army. His woman must have tried to get out for help and was drowned. I can't see no other way, or she'd have been down the river with a posse after what she left behind."

"Drowned?" his wife whispered, and that was almost the first word she had said to him. Her face was bitter, as if this was just another proof of the horror of this wild Texas land.

"I reckon you better ride along behind me now. I got to get this to Sugareet sure," he said gravely.

Her dull eyes rested on the bundle.

"It's her babe," he said.

"Drowned too?" she whispered.

"Mighty near," he agreed.

Her face twisted and grew cruel. "You mean it's still alive?"

"It was a little while ago."

"Coe Elliot!" she cried, sitting up. "Give it here to me!"

He handed over the bundle, staring at her. Now what do you suppose got into her? You never could make out women. About the time you figured you knew how they'd take to something, they'd take it a different way. He watched her lift the cloth off that small face. Those tiny eyes squinted from the daylight, the peaked face screwed up and the pale lick of a mouth started to cry.

"It's suffocated and most starved!" she cried at him. "Coe Elliot, go out and get it some fresh milk!"

Now wasn't that just like a woman, he told himself. Why, a cowman never got a taste of milk, unless he had a family and his wife kept a tame cow in the corral. He rode grimly up to the mesa on this side, where he had seen some Bar Cross T calves with their mammies not far off. He could tackle a cow here and still keep his eye on the wagon. Those cows looked peaceful enough grazing there in a bunch like a V, heads all one way, but he felt glad no cowhand was around to watch him.

Oh, he roped his cow easy, and his mare did what she could to keep the rope tight, but the mare had to dodge

The Flood

when that longhorn made a rush for her. And when the cow wasn't after his mount, she was swinging at him. He couldn't get a drop till he took a couple of dallies around a cedar with his rope and snubbed the cow fast. Then, while it bawled and jerked and kicked, his hands manfully did their bidding. The canteen mouth was mighty small, but he got what precious white wetness he could and hustled back to the wagon with it.

His young wife shook the canteen. "Is that all you got?" she cried.

"Ain't that enough?" he stammered.

It was the look she gave him, he told himself, that sent him across the river—a provoked, exasperated, belittling look for him as a milker. Anything bad that came out of this now was her fault, for he had nothing to say. Already that bunch of cows he had tackled on this side had drifted out of sight of the wagon. But a few grazed on the other side. They looked like grains of sand up on the escarpment. He could keep an eye on the wagon from there. She told him to take a tin cup along. He could milk into it better, she said, and pour from that into the canteen. He took it silently from her hand, but the rifle he left behind. It would be mighty unhandy swimming the deep channel.

Once out in the swift current, his eyes swept the rim of the escarpment ahead. The cap rock above him dipped with arroyos and was tufted with cedars. He had seen no fresh sign on the wagon side of the river, and if that pair of red devils that followed them lay up there with their ponies picketed in some hidden draw, he couldn't help it. He hadn't wanted to come to this side. He had no choice. It might be too far for a good shot from up there to the wagon, but it was mighty close range to where he was putting himself now.

Even then he wouldn't make like he cared when it first

happened. All he heard above the snorts and splashes of his swimming mare was a noise like the breaking of a distant corral bar. At the same time, he saw, just a little ahead of him, a gush of water raise from the river. It stood up for a moment, spinning like a top.

He had his cap-and-ball pistol in his belt, twice looped around his neck to keep it from the water, but all he could make out was a puff of black smoke floating away from the rim of the mesa. Then, nearer on the escarpment, another puff came. He could see the smoke before he heard the report. Almost at once, his mare sank and was gone, leaving him struggling in the water.

Well, it had happened like he thought, he told himself, and tried to swim back to the wagon. But the river bore him away. The main current ran as if something had given way in the narrows below, and all the water was going out. He kept his head above with difficulty. He hung to a piece of floating gatepost with one hand and worked for the wagon side of the river with the other all the time, but he was being swept downstream. When he saw it was hopeless, he raised up in the water as far as he could and tried to see Bethiah. He couldn't see her. Last thing he made out before the current swept him around the bend was two red riders swimming their ponies for the wagon. After a little, he heard what he never wanted to hear. The shots rang loudly several times along the bed of the water and echoed from escarpment to escarpment.

Far below and very far spent, he dragged himself out and stood in the shadow of a rock, blowing. All he could hear when he got his breath was the low gurgle of water and a curlew calling dismally as it flew over the flood in the dusk. Once he thought that he heard a horseman climbing the dim mesa. His pistol lay at the bottom of the river, but he still had his knife. He took the benefit of every shadow and bush as he made his way up the river. He could now see the wagon in the deepening gloom, a lone, desolate dot surrounded by the wide water. Save for the specks of oxen, it hadn't a sign of life about. But when he grew closer, he thought he smelled smoke, and as he came abreast on the shore, there rose a faint, sinister glow of red in the wagon.

Wading out in the darkness, he could tell the river was definitely lower. Now that the worst had happened to him, the flood was going down. The oxen must be still alive, he reckoned, for he could hear the constant creak of yoke and coupling ring. Once he felt sure he saw the moving shadow of someone against the wagon sheet. It looked like a woman.

He splashed loudly, so if Bethiah were there she might be warned of his coming. Instantly, a rifle cracked from the wagon and a bullet sang near him.

"Bethiah!" he called.

"Why didn't you say who it was?" she called back sharply. In a little while he pulled himself up over the front wheel.

That was a picture under the wagon sheet he reckoned he'd never see in this life, Bethiah and the babe big as life and kicking. His wife had set a dutch oven on a plank and had a low fire of wagon wood going in it. She must have opened her trunk, for she had changed her red dress for a blue homespun one. As he climbed in, she knelt there by her pappy's rifle while she boiled coffee and fried bacon. Her bedroll had been spread on the boards. On it a tin cup and plate for him had evidently just been laid. And down there in the water, a-watching everything, was the babe. She had bedded it in the cedar tub. And now that tub kept floating around the wagon box, rocking like a cradle in every little wave their movements in the wagon made.

"I might 'a' killed you like I did that red devil!" she scolded.

73

He looked at her. Her slight little face with its black hair parted in the middle and pulled down on both sides didn't look like she could take her part or stand her ground. But he knew better now.

"What happened to the other one?"

"He didn't stay," she said briefly.

Little by little, as he put out the fire, she told how she stood behind her pile of barrels and boxes to fire out of the wagon. She vowed she was going to get that other devil, for he had put an unsightly bullet hole in her trunk, and that meant through some of her best fixens. She'd have done it, too, for she could reload faster than he could. She had often done it for her pappy. But he turned tail and ran.

Coe sat there mighty quiet while they ate their supper, hardly daring to look at her, lest she see the respect in his eyes. Mostly he watched the babe in the tub swimming around the wagon. He had left a small, lone coal for light. So this was how a man felt when he was married, he told himself, with his wife cooking for him and setting beside him to eat while their young one drooled to itself close by. This was something to carry off in his mind with him to the war, something to come back to afterward. And if she could take care of a ranch like she could a wagon, he'd have something to come back to when it was over. "Water's goin' down fast," he told her when they finished. "That young one's tub'll ground in a minute. If this keeps on, the trail will be free by midnight. Maybe then we can get your oxen a-goin'."

The moon was just coming up as she washed the dishes and fed the babe for the night.

"You might as well get some sleep till the water's down," he told her. "I don't expect that long-haired feller to bother you any more tonight."

She didn't say anything right then. But when he went to get his bed, she said he needn't bother. She said it, looking

74

the other way. It was mighty narrow for a bed out there on the wagon seat. He could sleep better here on the platform, if he wanted to. Her bed, she allowed, was wide enough for two.

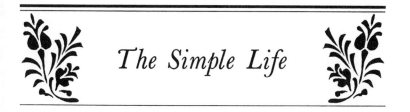

The Simple Life

Iᴛ's ɴᴇᴀᴛʟʏ ʙᴏᴜɴᴅ ᴀɴᴅ tamed with steel wire today, that free, open range Doane Williams used to know. And rushing headlights and revolving sky beacons break the loneliness of its night. The tide of progress flows on and never ebbs. Times have changed, even on the range. Life is complex now. But back in the horse-and-buggy days, they say, life was very simple then.

I wouldn't know, for the time Doane Williams came in a pole buggy to take my sister Rudith to the roundup wedding, I was only a chuckleheaded kid whose reading, writing and arithmetic lessons were marked up on horses' and cattle's sides. All I knew was that the fall roundup was moving east from the Arizona Territory line, with twenty-some outfits, nine wagons, a hundred hands and nearly half a thousand horses, with stray men combing the hills far north and south and sweeping down into the center of the net a tremendous herd of beef. And I wasn't along.

For six or seven weeks they had been driving toward the Rio Grande. Now they were nearly done. The biggest show on earth, that never could be put under canvas, was giving a last performance not thirty miles away. My father and his several hands were there, and all the boys and even girls from ranches along the line of march had ridden out, I knew, to eat with the men. But this year my mother said I was too young to go.

She waited until the last to tell me, and I felt the blood storm into my face.

"Milt Craig's only twelve years old!" I bawled. "And he's there, a-drawin' a man's wages!"

"You saw the calf roundup." She crossed the room in her matter-of-fact way and peered up at the medicine shelf. "I reckon you can stay home once."

"If pa was home, you wouldn't dare say that!"

"Your father's the one that told me to."

"If he did, you put him up to it!" I cried.

My mother took down a bottle and poured some green stuff in a tumbler. Her face, as she drank it, had a bitter look.

"You're too young a boy to see a man get shot down in cold blood. I won't have you calloused to that sort of business if I can help it."

"Nobody's a-goin' to get shot down in cold blood!" I yelled.

She turned on me quickly. "Hush up, and go out someplace," she warned in a low voice.

When I looked around, my sister Rudith was coming slowly out of her sleeping room, her face a little pale above the bright scraps of old dresses in her hands. You could see she had been piecing a quilt for the hope chest my father had made for her from the Chino trees in our hills. He'd had the small logs ripped over at Stevens' sawmill, and then smoothed the pretty red and white boards with his own jack plane.

"Who's going to get shot?" she asked.

I looked at my mother, but her face was hard and masked as a Navajo's.

"Nobody!" I said scornfully, and walked out.

Riding old Slag up on the Point of Rocks where his bare feet could hold better than shod ones, I could see far across the San Augustine plains a pillar of yellow cloud rising and drifting against the blue fall sky. It was like a huge, beckoning hand. Over there where that dust was rising were life and excitement with horses and men. I couldn't take my eyes off of it, and that evening on the corral fence I kept watching the low red stars of the distant roundup fires winking through the dark. Over there, I knew, men were eating a late supper and talking in their blankets, and the night guards were riding around the cattle, singing to quiet them down. I couldn't stand it. The wind came softly in my face, and I thought I could detect across the plains the smell of roundup cooking, the best in the world. My mother kept calling to me: Where was I, what was I doing and why didn't I come in?

I went in at last when she started coming for me with a bull's-eye lantern, but I couldn't sleep. Long before daylight I was up and pulling on my pants and shirt and calfskin vest. When I got outside I pulled on my boots. Cherry, my red mare, was at the bars for me when I reached the corral. I bridled and saddled her, cinching her tight. Then we set out in the dark plains night. I didn't need to dig a knee or jerk a rein. She knew where I was going as well as I did and headed straight for a bright morning star that I knew must hang over where the roundup lay.

There are things in a boy's life he never forgets, and what I saw when I rode over the last rise next morning was a sea rolling and tossing with Texas steers. Oh, there were blues, duns, creams and slates, blacks with bay points, speckled reds, line-backs and pintos, some with white spectacles or stars, old mossy heads out of the hills with wide, upturned horns eight feet and more from tip to tip, a few scattered bulls and dry cows, and a sprinkling of roan Durhams, blackpoll Anguses and humped Brahmas. But most of them were longhorns with plenty of light under their bellies and with legs that could carry them to market if that had to be.

Some brands had already been cut and were being held

in small herds. But it was still the big show in full swing, with the cattle bawling and milling, their bodies fitted snug as sardines, their heads held high above. Horns were clacking. Hands were changing saddles to fresh horses. Riders were cutting out heifers and all cows with late, missed calves, and turning back bunch-quitting steers. And through the dust and din men rawhided one another as they passed.

"Nick, I never saw you miss somebody else's calf when you and him was out in the brush."

"All right. All right. It's yourn, you ole cow thief."

"I seen many a chew of tobacker get kicked out of a man for steppin' off a hoss like that."

"Ever meet a terrapin, Tom? I know you never overtook one."

"You claim this one, Telesphor?"

"I don't claim nothin'," the Mexican said sullenly, for you can't charge a man with stealing if he doesn't claim the Rafter SP he had changed to his Diamond 8B.

"You done a good job," Booger Johnson, of the Rafter SP's, twitted him. "I was a-goin' to give him to you."

Oh, things were just like always. The smoke rose peacefully by the nine or ten wagons standing with open bows in the *cañada*. And Sandy McCune, one of our hands, winked hard to me as he rode past on the tail of a white-footed steer.

Then my father saw me, and I wasn't so sure. He trotted up and his eyes, red-rimmed with dust, looked at me sternly.

"I thought you was to stay home!"

"You never told me," I choked.

My father was a little chunky man with a sorrel cast and scaly skin. He started to say something harsh, checked it, and his eyes ran over the roundup as if they had been drawn to a certain figure many times before. My eyes followed his; but even before his glance found its man, I knew who it would be.

"Go over to the wagon and get your dinner," he ordered me. "Then you can start home."

I closed my lips tightly. He couldn't send me off like that. My mare had to rest up overnight anyhow, before she'd be good for the trip. But my father read my mind. "I'll see you get a fresh hoss," he said shortly.

He rode off and my eyes went back to the man he had looked at. It was Doane Williams in a check shirt, and California britches tucked in his boots, which in those days came close to every man's knees. He was on a bony blue roan, and Tom Camber, on a smooth black, was facing him not two yards away. The dust had drifted like gray snow on Doane's hat, eyebrows and young mustaches, silvering them, but that semblance of old age couldn't hide the young snap in his chin or the reckless glitter in his good-humored, dark eyes. There, across a sea of longhorn backs, he sat his saddle as easy as a bunkhouse bench, and yet there was something in the angle of his boyish back that stiffened me. Oh, I made a try to ride off to the wagons, like my father said, but from both sides of the herd I saw riders drifting closer to watch and listen, and I drifted, too, keeping behind the mounted bulk of old white-bearded Cap Griscom, so my father wouldn't see me. But Sandy found me, and his flea-bitten gray cut my red mare easy as a heifer out of the herd and kept pushing her till she and I were far outside.

"I want to see what's going on!" I yelled angrily.

"They ain't nothin' a-goin' on," he came back easy. "Only two hands talkin' over a pied steer."

I knew he was lying, for Doane Williams was no hand. He was wagon boss of the Box Bars at eighteen, and Colonel Twyman had made him foreman before he died. The boy foreman, some called him. And Tom Camber was no hand either. He owned and ran the middling small TC's. They said he had to leave Texas, but Booger Johnson joked around it couldn't be so, for the sheriff had come to the New Mexico line and begged him to come back. My father said Camber had shot two Negroes, but you'd never know it to go in his ranch house and see him sitting there like a woman, braiding fancy quirts with his white fingers. That was his pastime and his hands were mighty deft and fast. He was sweet on Rudith and gave her a pair of quirts, one for plain riding and one for fancy. She was mighty proud of them. But she wouldn't have anything more to do with Tom Camber than before.

"You better eat something," Sandy told me, and Boiling William, our cook, fed me promptly. Till I was done, Sandy came riding in from the *remuda* with a smoky blue that we called Railroad because of his Double R brand. Sandy changed my saddle and bridle and said he'd side me part-way home.

Oh, I knew my father told him to make sure I went home and didn't sneak back. We rode hours without saying a word, like a deputy and his cow-thief prisoner, but I was thinking hard in my mind something the butcher at Magdalena had told around—how one time Camber sold him some steers, and Shultz showed him six calves and beeves in the stockyard he was going to slaughter. Camber pulled out his six-shooter and Shultz said he heard only one long shot, but the six-shooter was empty and the six beasts lay on the ground shot through the head.

"You ain't missed nothin'," Sandy told me when we could see our house. "Tamest roundup I seen yet."

He was trying to pull wool over my eyes, I knew, and I kept my mouth bitterly closed.

"Nothin' but work," Sandy went on. "Two suppers every night. One after dark and the other plenty before sunup.

The Simple Life

Night before last, Cap Griscom asked could he fetch any-thing back from town. Nick Waggoman said, yes, he could. He'd like to trade his bed for a lantern."

But I wouldn't crack a smile.

"Well," he drawled, "I got to rustle back now and get to work. Tell your ma they're quittin' Saturday for Kate Oldaker's dance and weddin'. That's the only reason your pa sent you home."

My mother came out to the corral to meet me, her face hard, as it was sometimes when I figured I could be no kin of hers.

"So you're back? You can fetch that pack in and put it under my bed. I don't want you running off again."

I did as she said without opening my mouth. That surprised her. She gave me a sharp sidewise glance.

"Everybody all right?"

I looked up and saw that Rudith was listening by the door.

"Who wouldn't be all right?" I came back rough as I dared. "Tamest roundup I ever been at. I wouldn't 'a' stayed if they paid me wages."

The funny thing was that before I had been home an hour I began to believe it myself. When I thought back over what I had seen, it seemed pretty flat. Nothing had really happened. For all I knew, Doane and Camber had been just talking over a pied steer. I had made a mountain out of a dog hole. Certainly this was the most peaceful day I could remember at home. The sunlight lay yellow as gold on the cottonwoods around the house. The sky hung clear and blue. Calves lay in the dust on the sunny side of the corral.

I went to bed telling myself that my mother's fool fretting had put things in my head that weren't so. Then next morning I woke up with the low, filing hum of men's voices in my ear.

83

I pulled on my pants and put one eye to a door crack. There were my father and Clem Fugatt with my mother in the kitchen. They must have ridden most of the night.

"I was standin' right by Doane when he done it," Clem said.

"Done what?" My mother's face had that fearful, bitter look.

"You can't altogether blame a young feller," Clem explained. "He'd been working hard six or seven weeks and had to get some of the snap out of him. All the time we were on the Box Bar range, Tom Camber was ridin' him. Tryin' to scare up a fight. If it wasn't this steer he claimed, it was that. He swore he knowed one speckled Box Bar branded calf when it had a TC mammy."

"Go on." My mother's grim mouth told that she knew those were fighting words.

"Doane took it all," my father put in hastily. "Never rared up once."

"I reckon now he was waitin' till we moved off his range," Clem said. "Then he figured he'd lack responsibility. Yesterday was his last day as roundup boss. Before dark he rode to his headquarters for a couple hours and got cleaned up. I guess he's comin' here today to take your Rue to the dance. Anyway, when he come back to the roundup he had a burlap roll behind him on the saddle. He took it over where Camber was sitting by his fire. You wouldn't guess they'd been anything between them. Doane was sweet and mild as barnyard milk."

"He said he had a hide that ought to make good whang leather," my father put in. "Said he'd give it to him—if Camber promised not to look at the brand."

"Go on." My mother wet her lips.

"Most everybody figured Doane was sweetenin' him up—a-crawlin' to him," Clem explained. "Camber must have too. He grinned a little and said he wouldn't pay no attention to the brand. Soon as Doane rode off he opened it up, and 'twas his own brand."

"What should that surprise Tom Camber for?" my mother came back sharply. "Does he eat his own brand? Does anybody you know of? . . . Do you, Clem?"

"That's not it, Angie," my father said.

"I may eat your brand, Miz Farnham," Clem flushed, "but I don't throw the hide in your face when I've done eating."

My father shook his head. "What Doane would want to do such a thing for, I can savvy. But what he went and done it for is beyond me."

"If he was lookin' for trouble, he sure picked the right man." Clem's leathery face was plenty sober. "But maybe he can't help it. It's in some's blood."

My mother's face looked cruel and she wiped her eyes. I knew what she was thinking. My father had said more than once that the Williamses were a strange family, for all the menfolks had met violent deaths but Doane. His father had died in the Lincoln County war; and Stacey and Frank, the oldest and the youngest, were shot over pre-emption rights to a spring. It was wintertime and Frank had a coat on, and those that saw it said the balls passing through his belly plopped out the coat behind. Then Matt, the curly-headed one, had gambled with death over a monte table and lost.

The murderer lost, too, for the Socorro County district attorney took his cattle, everybody said, to split the jury the first time and then took his ranch to get a self-defense verdict the second time. And the vigilantes hanged him that night in Death Alley. But that didn't bring Matt back.

Clem Fugatt must have been thinking much the same thing. His cheeks had flattened.

"Your Rue can ride to my place today, Miz Farnham, and go to the weddin' with my Julie tomorrow. I mean if you don't want her ridin' with Doane, in case they meet Camber—"

"Sh!" my mother said.

Back in the hallway I heard the door to my sister's sleeping room open and then I saw her come out in the kitchen fully dressed. Her face was a little pale, as it had been a good bit lately, but I knew, by the calm look in her eyes, she hadn't been sneak enough to listen like I had. Her braids hung soft and brown down her back. And right then I knew I didn't want to see how she took it when they told her. I pulled on my boots and the rest of my clothes and crawled out the window. I was sitting bareback on old Slag up in Water Draw when I saw her ride off with old Clem Fugatt, a roll of clothes for the wedding dance tied behind her on the sidesaddle. She rode erect and quiet, making no fuss that I could see or hear, but I knew what she thought and felt.

Whenever I came in the ranch house that day, I could feel the shadow of the cloud that hung over it. And when I rode up on the Point of Rocks that afternoon I could see a second cloud coming to meet it, a handful of dust far out on the San Augustine plains and stirred up by a black speck. Sometimes that speck would be swallowed up by the earth, then it would bob up again like a dark cork from some unseen slough or *cañada*, while other smaller specks raced to cross in front of it, for reasons best known to antelope themselves.

It was close to suppertime when that dust rolled up to our ranch door, and there was a pole buggy with green cushions and Doane Williams spruced up in a town haircut, a clean blue shirt and his sun-faded California britches bright and new in the lower legs, where they had been pulled out of his boots and down outside, as befitted a formal occasion. It was plain from the rig that he had ridden forty-seven miles last night to the livery stable at Magdalena, then driven fifty-two miles across country to our place today and still had some thirty miles to go tomorrow, which was about a hundred and thirty miles to take his girl in style to a dance that was only eight or ten miles from where he was in the first place.

"Why, howdy, Doane," my father said, coming out of the house. "You're gettin' sporty. Light and come in. I'll put your team away."

If Doane was surprised to see a man he'd left last night at the roundup, he gave no sign. I could tell my father wanted to be out while my mother broke the news that Rue wasn't there, and why, and much as I liked to be near Doane and take in every move he made, I stayed out, too, helping to make a long rite out of a short chore. I still hated to go in when my father did, but I hadn't need to. Doane was in the kitchen. He had one of my mother's aprons on, and was mixing dough in a yellow bowl.

"Doane makes such good biscuits," my mother said. "I asked him to help me out, since Boiling William's away."

"I don't mind, Miz Farnham," Doane said. "I ain't been doin' anything all day."

He moved around the stove, quiet and easy, with never a useless motion. He was calm as could be, but I knew my mother had told him everything and begged him to stay away from the dance and wedding, but it hadn't done any good, for her face had that cruel, convulsed look some get just before and after they break into tears. I saw Doane look up at her once or twice. His own face was grave as any cowhand's, but his dark eyes looked full of snap and dance, like they always did.

"I ever tell you, Miz Farnham, about the time Alice Morris came out to the roundup and said she'd give us French dressin'? All the boys ate their plates clean and none of them said a word. Then she found she'd used the cook's bottle of skunk oil instead of her olive oil. 'Why didn't you tell me?' she said. Booger Johnson said, 'Well, it tasted kinda funny, Miss Alice, but that's the way I figured French dressin' was.' "

"I never heard that one," my mother said.

Doane rolled the lumps of dough deftly in a tin of warm tallow and set them by the stove to rise. He squinted a practiced eye through the lid hole at the fire.

"But the time you'd 'a' laughed, Miz Farnham," he went on, "was the last I heard Miz Bonnefoy gave cowhands coats to eat in. You know she'd been to El Paso and every place, and men hadn't dare sit in their shirt sleeves at her table. Well, we got there before noon and got asked in. You know what a short feller Hardy is. She gave him a little bitty coat. Now, I got kinda long arms, and she gave me the biggest one she had. Well, when she went out of the room, Hardy and me changed coats and then went in to dinner. My coat hung up around my withers and hardly come to my elbows, and Hardy's sleeves fell down over his hands and got in the soup. The hired maid snickered around the table. Oh, it was a circus till it was done."

My mother gave a little snort in her throat, but my father didn't laugh. He was staring at Doane. Here he was, not much more than a boy and less than twenty-four hours away from Tom Camber's gun, and cheering up a woman, so she wouldn't embarrass him by worrying about him. I can taste that supper as if it was only today. We ate in the kitchen with the good smell from the oven and the snap of burning cedar wood from the stove and the pleasant sound of Doane's easy voice in our ears, telling us some of the cheerful news he heard on the range since he saw us last. His biscuits had come out light as a feather, as only hot sourdough biscuits can, and my mother kept saying how good they were, but I noticed she hardly ate any.

The Simple Life

All the time Doane talked, it seemed she was listening more to something in her own mind than to what he said, though she kept her eyes on him. I think we all looked a lot at Doane Williams that night. There he sat under the soft light from the oil lamp, with its yellow paper shade scorched through in several places, more boyish and enjoying life than I could remember, his yellow mustaches fair and young and his dark eyes full of dance and sparkle.

And that's the memory he left with us the next morning when it was barely daylight, as he got in his livery pole buggy and shook the lines over Midnight and Slippers and waved to us as he drove off. You couldn't help notice that he hadn't asked any of us to ride along, though he had a half-empty buggy and we ourselves were leaving soon after. Much as my mother feared to go, she could never stay away from Kate Oldaker's wedding and dance now.

Before we left, I went into Rudith's room to steal one of her fancy silk neckerchiefs to wear. As I came in, Doane and his three brothers stared back at me from her high bureau. The picture had been taken in front of Bartlett and Tyler's store in Magdalena, with the four in flat hats and tight britches, and the gun of Frank, the youngest, buckled on, rustler fashion. Today, as always when I saw it, I thought how pictures of dead people looked as if they had been doomed to die from the start. Already in the faces of those boys the seeds of destruction had been sown. They stood there staring with strange eyes at the camera, as if in the dark hole of the lens they saw the likeness to a six-shooter barrel and in the wrinkled black cloth over the photographer's head the symbol of a shroud.

All the way to the Diamond D's that day, my mother sat stiffly erect on her hard buckboard seat, and her cheeks had the cast of those cut from gyp rock. The wheel tracks kept rolling in wide sweeping curves, first to one side and then the other, but her face was set directly ahead for Kate

Oldaker's wedding. My father rode the smoky horse, Rail-road. He followed behind mostly, letting us set the pace, and the few times he rode abreast or passed to the lead, his face was no more communicative than hers. Scarcely a word was spoken between us, even when we nooned at a dry camp and hung our cut, gunny-sack *morals* on the horses' heads, eating the lunch my mother had fetched along in the buckboard with the small sack of oats and the flour sack of my father's best clothes for the wedding.

Late in the afternoon we climbed the last ridge. The silver tops of the Diamond D windmills came slowly into view, then the entire ranch, lying close to the foothills. And now, two or three miles out on the plain, we could see the herd drifting in a kind of great V to graze, and held by men who didn't give a hoot to go to a wedding. Our horses trotted down the last hill. My mother thrust up her bosom several times in that fortifying manner of hers and smoothed her face, for soon she'd have to greet and laugh with people she hadn't seen for six months or a year.

It looked as safe and peaceable around the ranch as an afternoon in town. The ground between bunkhouse, stable, blacksmith shop and corrals was dotted with buckboards, spring wagons, a few buggies and heavy wagons. All stood around empty. Harnesses hung from the swingletrees. Some saddles lay where careless riders had dumped them, though more had been set carefully on the top rail of the corral, where they swam like big brown ducks in a row. Here and there around the barbecue pit men squatted in groups, drawing diagrams of trails, brands and places in the dust and swapping news and saddle-packed bottles.

"Aren't those men from the TC's?" my mother asked in a low voice.

"Looks like it," my father said shortly.

Over the hills from the direction of the Box Bars we could make out Doane riding one of Sam Oldaker's mounts.

When he got close we saw he held up a bunch of red and white geraniums in his hand.

"Kate's bride's flowers didn't come from El Paso," he said. "Miz Twyman reckoned I better fetch some from her house plants."

His snapping black eyes scrutinized my mother to see how she was taking the presence of the TC men at the wedding. There they squatted, harmless looking as any other hands, except that they kept watch on the country out of the tail of their eyes. An outlaw, everybody knew, could always get a job with the TC's. Camber claimed they made the best hands that were. Well, my father said, he expected they did. A man who was wanted never stayed long enough to start his own brand. He wouldn't say no to riding the roughest, loneliest pinnacles, where honest cowhands didn't hanker to go. Seldom if ever did he want to knock off work to go to town.

Doane held up the flowers for my mother to sniff the sweet smell of the crunched leaves.

"Nelse Fielding and his seven head of young ones comin'," he said cheerfully. "On two hosses over in the next draw. Nelse ever tell you, Miz Farnham, how he had to hold the lamp at his own weddin'? Down in Texas, it was. They was only him and his bride and the preacher. When the preacher started readin' the marriage words, Nelse's hand shook so the preacher had to stop. He lost his place and Nelse told me he didn't believe they ever were married, but got baptized instead."

My mother's face brightened. She seemed good as any time now. I looked around, but if there was any sign of Tom Camber's saddle, I couldn't make it out. It would be a big fifty-pound saddle, hand-worked and with braided loops down over the horn. It wasn't here. Perhaps, I thought, he didn't intend coming and had sent some of his men just for the looks of it. At the thought, the Diamond D's grew suddenly brighter, and I was pleasantly aware, as if for the first time, of the good smell of browning beef, the solid reassurance of the log walls, the peaceful chattering of windmills and the lively yells of boys and girls playing among the rigs. Even the dark, slaty clouds that had been pushing out from the mountaintops all day looked lighter. I helped my father unhitch the team and turn it into the horse pasture, then followed him to the bunkhouse, where he hung up his gun belt with the rest and started to pull off his chaps and pants to change for the wedding.

Our Sandy had seen us from the ranch-house gallery. His bowlegs came musically in the bunkhouse. He wore bell spurs and liked to draw each one, as he walked, along the other pants leg. I thought he gave my father a slow look.

"How'd you like," he said to me, "to sleep out at the wagon with me tonight?"

I shook my head.

"Your mare's homesick to see you."

"I don't want to," I said.

I saw him lift a keen blue glance out of the open doorway and over the hills. Then I went outside.

The men seemed a little quiet, I thought, for a wedding, but there was nothing like that among the women. When I went in the big front door at dusk, the house was noisy as a calf corral. The hall was a great dim room twelve feet wide by thirty long, with pine settees on the side and tanned burro and calfskins on the floor. Steer horns hung above most every doorway. In one room babies and small children were being put to bed, and in the next two you could hear older girls and women gabbing as they washed and dressed and rolled up their hair in rusty curlers that I knew they heated in oil lamps. The clatter of a sewing machine came from another room, where Mrs. Toble, who lived back in the Red Lake country among the Navajos, was desperately trying to make two dresses in time for the wedding; one for herself and another out of the same piece for her little girl, who stood by, ugly as sin with her hair braided so tight back over her head that her eyes stuck out.

But the liveliest room was the kitchen, with the women helping the men cooks. Some were icing the bride's cake and taking out of the oven the last batches of dried-apple and peach pies. Some were cutting up the barbecued meat. And some had the big black roundup coffeepots ready on the fire.

The men were starting to straggle into the big front room by way of the hall now. They looked a little stiff in their best stovepipe pants pulled out of their boots. There were fine wedding decorations of pine branches on the fireplace mantel. The river preacher turned up the wick of his lamp high as he could to read by. And now Mrs. Toble had to give up the sewing machine and come in, with her and her little girl's new dresses mostly basted and stuck together with pins.

Out in the hall, Billy Carney was waiting for the bride to come out of the room where they had fixed her up. Now somebody was coming in and all the women were standing up with the men. It was Billy and his bride. He walked in little steps, like all cowpunchers whose feet are too small from no more exercise than they can get in a stirrup. He had on a long coat with tails, but the woman in creamy white from neck to floor beside him and carrying a bunch of red and white geraniums in her hand didn't look at all like the Kate Oldaker I knew, who could cut out a calf any day, and hogtie and brand it as good as a man. Yet my mother looked after her with rapt wet eyes.

"Christian friends!" The river preacher's voice boomed back from the beams as solemn as from church rafters. "We are gathered here in the aims of holy matrimony."

There was more commotion back by the hall door. I was too short to see what it was and had to get it secondhand from my mother's face. Without moving her head, her eyes swept back to the rear of the room. Then the fond look faded and her eyes settled with tragic import across the room to Rudith.

The crowd was opening up with too much alacrity to suit me. Over the shaggy heads of several half-grown boys, I saw pushing a fine high forehead mounted with wavy combed hair. The head was lifted back with a very noble look, free-handed, open and generous, and yet there was something in the pale skin and brilliant eyes that belied it. The boys moved hastily aside and Tom Camber stood there in a little circle of elbowroom and a tight-fitting black coat. The high lapels would have buttoned up close to his neck. The coat was open and you could see his gun belt had been hung up in the bunkhouse with the others. But something under his pants belt and the lower part of his vest bulged out just in front of his right hip.

I didn't listen to a word the river preacher said that day, but I can still hear his voice droning off marriage words and see those roundup haircuts of the men and the stillness of the women. Rudith was staring at this wedding that, for Billy and Kate, would end happily enough, with Billy riding the cattle train with the Diamond D steers to the Missouri and Kate following by passenger coach for a honeymoon back East in Kansas City. How it would end for Rudith was something else. You could see the look in her face. But Doane stood there easy and boyish, so you could hardly bear to look at him. And when the river preacher said that Billy and Kate were one, Doane called out high words for the bride as lighthearted as anybody.

"Get him out of here!" I saw my mother's lips move to my father.

He made as if he didn't hear and, young as I was, I knew my mother didn't really expect him to. She had only spoken out of her heart for Rudith. Men died this way most every day in the territory, and neither my father nor any man could mix into it beforehand. That was the code. Even a girl out in our country saddled up her own horse. She might reckon she knew the string better than she did and pick out an outlaw she couldn't rope or ride if she did, but unless she came right out and asked for it, no man would insult her by offering help. Much less would any man offend Doane. Oh, I knew most of the men and women felt for him and some, like Rudith or my mother, might bleed for him, but that was as far as another was welcome to go. Doane would tend to his own business, and if he went down, it would be like all the Williamses, with a smile on his lips and the devil in his eye.

Before ten men had kissed the bride—and hands were good as owners in a cow camp—Stuttering Bob had his fiddle up to his chin, and was jerking out a square-dance version of "Muley Bull in the Canebrake." Old Man Waite tuned his strings and Johnny Romero sat, smiling, back in his chair and started softly weaving a bright undertone with his guitar.

"Clear the floor, ladies and gents!" Tod Granger sang out, for now a caller, and not a preacher, was running the outfit. He was raw and hollow-looking, and wore a surcingle with three buckles for a belt. "Them that's empty can go in to supper. Them that ate this mawnin' can shake a leg."

I knew Tod was a friend of Doane's, but you wouldn't think so. Most of those in the room jumped at the excuse to get away from Doane and Tom Camber. Oh, my mother didn't go, nor Rudith either, although she was a good friend of Kate's and was expected to eat at the first table. And Doane made for Rudith for the first dance, like all was sweet as 'lasses and wild lilac. But there was something like imploring terror in Rudith's eyes as she signaled him before he reached her. She couldn't dance with him. Not tonight.

Booger Johnson saw how the land lay and stepped to help her out. "Pardner for the dance, Miss Rue?"

She took his arm. Her cheeks had the peculiar color of the chamiso that grows in the draws. I never saw her look prettier, in her wine-red dress that had a kind of jacket with black velvet trimmings, her hair done up soft and brown in curls, and a gay silk handkerchief Doane himself had given her tucked in at her neck and caught up at the waist.

I expected Doane to stare at her and maybe look hurt or flare up, but he just stopped easy as could be and turned to Sally Abercrombie, who was dark and Scotch.

"You and me ain't danced this long time, Miss Sally?" he asked her.

Tom Camber was on the other side of the room. There were plenty empty benches and settees now, but he stood there by himself, not ten feet from the door and not a sign on his face that he took notice of the trouble they had to get two more sets of dancers in the big front room, although it was none at all to get three out in the hall, which would crowd it.

Tod stood in the doorway, where he could keep both rooms going at the same time.

"Salute your pardners!" he called.

Fiddlers and fiddlers' feet were moving in earnest now. Stuttering Bob sat there with one tight pants leg crossed over the other and his head cocked back and lids half-lowered, as if watching the effect of his music on savage breasts, while Tod Granger made up the most outrageous calls with no more smile than if he were looking down in his dead mother's grave:

> *"Swing her if you like her, round and round,*
> *Pockets full of rocks to hold you down.*
>
> *Bow to that gent and bump him on the head.*
> *If he don't like biscuits, give him corn bread."*

The Simple Life

In both front room and long hall now, men's cow boots and ladies' hightop shoes were clicking. Couples were bowing, sashaying, taking arms, turning, whirling, stepping backward and forward, joining hands and circling, breaking and swinging. And all the while, over Booger's arm or shoulder, Rudith's eyes begged Doane to understand. It wasn't getting hurt herself that she was afraid of. No, it was he. If he danced with her tonight, it would only aggravate Tom Camber. She'd do anything she could to pacify Tom Camber tonight.

Oh, everybody there knew why she was doing it—everybody except Doane. His strong boyish face still held to its easy good humor. He sallied the other dancers when they passed and swung the girls impartially till their full skirts stood out and the buttons tried to fly off their tight basques. But those who reckoned Doane didn't mind, knew different before the night was over.

When midnight passed and nothing had happened, people began to breathe easier. It looked as if it might blow over after all, and it was no trouble to fill the big front room with dancers now. By two o'clock Johnny Romero looked tired and Stuttering Bob sat there fast asleep, playing "Rye Whisky" just as good as if awake. But nobody else was even gappy. All night the big black coffeepots had been kept hot on the fire and there was always a bunch out there eating a snack. Doane had hardly missed a dance. He showed the Varsoviana to a girl from Missouri, saying to her as he danced, "Put your little foot, put your little foot, put your little foot right there." And when everybody else dropped out of a strenuous Mexican polka, he and Bob Hooker yelled to the fiddlers to keep on and kept jumping and bobbing for twenty minutes more to see who could outlast the other.

Yes, it looked like there was a good chance now that it would blow over. Then those two commission men from

Socorro had to get Doane in a corner and ask him for a price on Box Bar steers, for old lady Twyman had left the shipping and selling to Doane since the colonel had died.

"Eighteen dollars," Doane told them.

"Isn't that a little steep?" the big one said. He had an ivory steer head for a watch charm. . . . "How about having one?"

And that's when most everybody found out that Doane minded what Rudith had done to him a lot more than he ever let on outside. He tipped the bottle up, and I thought he would never bring it down. Three times after that I saw Rudith waltz by that corner with her big eyes in a white face begging him, but he never looked up at her once.

"What do you say about those steers now," the big commission man said.

"Nineteen-fifty," Doane told him.

The big commission man looked at the little one with the red-dotted vest, and the latter went out and brought in more cheer. If they had a good time before, it was nothing to what they had now. Doane lifted the second bottle plenty times and I could see his Adam's apple work up and down.

"We're all friends together, Mr. Williams," the big commission man said at last. "Let's make a deal and shake on it. What's the best you can make on those steers?"

Doane handed the bottle back. "Twenty dollars—to my friends!" he sang out.

Somebody—I think it was young Ray Morley—laughed out loud. The two commission men tried to hold Doane there, but he pushed them back like paper men and got to his feet. He was steady as a picket pin. You couldn't tell he was any different now, except he might have been quieter than he had been.

They were dancing a schottische. Will I ever forget it? Three steps and a kick, then three steps and a swing. Stuttering Bob was out in the kitchen for a snack of coffee, and Vince Byrnes from the Double H's had taken his place with a mouth harp. Mrs. Toble was dancing with the bald-headed cook of the Muleshoes. Stays stuck out from behind her shoulder and every now and then her partner would give a jerk as he came in contact with a pin. Her dress had long since started coming apart where it had been basted. Now it was so bad she had to hold it together as she hopped, while watchers along the wall said it was her last dance—she'd have to go to bed after this.

Old Ben Mitchell said afterward he knew then that Doane had had enough of this monkey business, for he heard him tell Cal Moss to look after the Box Bar steers to Kansas City, and this is what he said: "Mossy, you might remember you ain't Noah and can't keep your stock on board forty days and nights. The law only gives you twenty-six hours. After that, you and Noah'll both go to jail."

Then he faced the floor and stood looking over the scene. For the last ten minutes you could hear, above the music and shuffling feet, the approaching rumble of fall mountain thunder. Doane kept standing there as if he was looking for somebody in particular. Finally his eyes fell on Camber, and he started across the floor.

"Now it's a-comin'!" I heard Gus Grostead say.

A pair of dancers noticed Doane's face and looked where he was headed for. Promptly they shied away. It didn't take long for others to give him plenty of room after that. Had Stuttering Bob been there with his fiddle it might have been different, for Bob would have kept on fiddling, hell or high water. He had played once clean through a fire, claiming it had caught him in a tight place and he couldn't stop. But Stuttering Bob was out in the kitchen, hitting the black coffee, and the other players couldn't take their eyes off Doane and the man who was waiting for him. The music dragged and dwindled, and that told the dullest dancers that something was wrong. And when the fiddle lost heart altogether, the last couples started hurrying off the floor.

You could hear the rain on the roof now, and loud laughing somewhere in the rest of the house. Soon enough they must have grown aware of the silence in here, for, room by room, the great ranch house grew quiet. Only a baby cried now. Up in the mountains the fall thunder cracked closer and you could hear it roll long over the foothills and plain. When I looked around, a dozen faces were watching from the two doorways.

I saw my mother making frantic motions for me to come, but I pretended not to see her. Everybody was off the floor now—everybody but Doane. His face was as grave and intent as a boy's. He took his time in those short stilted steps of a man who spent too much time in the saddle. His heels made hard clicks across the slicked floor.

Then he stopped in front of his enemy.

"Howdy, Tom," he drawled. "You havin' a good time?"

Camber stood with his back against the wall, watching him, not knowing exactly what was behind this.

Doane went on cheerfully, "No, you ain't havin' a good time. You won't dance. You won't eat. What in hell did you come here for?"

Tom Camber's eyes burned. "Get your gun," he said in a voice so low I couldn't get it, but I heard afterward what he said. "And I'll kill you in six places."

Doane's face brightened as if it had reminded him of something pleasant. "I ever tell you, Tom, about the Driskell boy that yelled he was killed in six places? He had got in a fight down in San Marcial. They fetched the doctor and found six bullet holes all right, but they were in Old Man Kane's buggy top. Well, every time Old Man Kane saw young Driskell after that, he asked him how he felt in his six bullet holes. The Driskell boy yelled the next time he said it he'd fix the old man. He did, too, on the hip. Old Man Kane said, 'He wouldn't 'a' hit me, but I thought he had a five-shooter and I only dodged five times.' "

Nobody laughed. The free, open, generous look on Tom Camber's face was almost gone. His mouth and eyes were something I had never quite seen before. But Doane stood there as pleased as a boy with new red-top boots, though his eyes were dark and mocking.

"Wait a minute," he said suddenly, and went out.

He was back before the older men could get their heads together, too soon to have gone to the bunkhouse. Some claimed his gun still hung in its scabbard in the bunkhouse next morning and that it was only a short horn he had stuck under his pants belt and vest, so no one could accuse him of taking a coward's shelter behind the lack of a gun. It bulged out in front of his right hip like Camber's did. My mother said afterward, it was plain he cared nothing for his life. Camber had picked him out, Rudith had gone back on him and he saw no way out of it but this.

He crossed the floor, and the stillness made his easy voice sound louder: "No, I can't feel sorry none for you, Camber. But I can for Billy and Kate. This here's their weddin' night. A weddin' night only comes once in a mighty long while. And me and you are breakin' it up—a-spoilin' it for them. If you come here so danged set on doin' something, why in hell don't you do it?"

Camber began to back toward the hall door. Two of his TC hands moved out behind him. Doane turned to face the three. He made a picture others who had been there told me, years afterward, they could still see, young and fine as they come, straight from the saddle, his head thrown back in that Western, exultance-over-Death look, a little crooked Williams smile twisting his mouth. And all around I had a glimpse of those cruel, bleak faces that meant unspoken grief in a man those days, and in many a woman.

"Not down in the belly where they got Frank!" Doane jeered. "Up here!" He jerked his empty right hand toward his left side, where the yellow strings of a tobacco sack hung down from his upper vest pocket.

The lightning winked bright as doomsday and the thunder fell, a quick, single crack. Even then, my mother said, it was strange that nobody thought of the herd. Here we all were, the men fresh from the roundup, and any chuckleheaded kid so small he needed a wagon wheel to crawl on a horse's back knew that a storm could scatter the work of weeks to the hills and brush. But all we could think of tonight was Doane and Camber and how it came out. In the hall several women screamed, thinking the thunder was something worse, and a good many in the room didn't know which it was for a mighty long moment.

I saw old Ben Mitchell, his face scarred like a butte, with one horny palm ready to come down on a smoking hot lamp chimney so Camber mightn't see so good. But he must have decided he hadn't need to. Afterward some said night before last was too long ago for a grudge over a beef to hold to the shooting stage, but that could hardly be true, for Camber had been given plenty fresh affront tonight. Most thought that Doane, with only a short horn for a gun and the sand of the Williamses, had backed him down for a minute. And before that minute was over, somebody was out in the hall, and the next we knew, Lou Knapp, not knowing what was up, came busting in. His black hat was rolling rain down on his shining yellow slicker.

It was plain he could see nothing wrong or didn't want to, for he threw a half-angry look around—the look of a man who has been working all night out in the cold and rain while his fellows enjoyed light and warmth indoors. "If you cowhands want any cattle tonight," he called, full of scorn as a toad, "you better come out and hold 'em!"

That broke it up. Men started running between Camber and Doane. The bridegroom forgot his bride. Even Stuttering Bob left his fiddle behind and went loping energetically off. Somebody fetched the cook's lantern to the gallery, but the men didn't need it. They had found their horses before on the blackest nights, and their saddles too. I caught sight of a figure running with widely bowed legs.

"Sandy!" I yelled. "You said I could go out to the herd with you tonight!"

He paid me no attention and I strung after, snatching a bridle from our buggy and trying to fix the line as I ran. It took me longer, for I had to find one of our buckboard horses in the pasture. I rode out bareback, letting my mount pick his way after the other horses. The rain slapped my face. Once away from the house it was dark as Egypt, but you could tell, by the popping of horns and the bellowing, when you got near the herd. The yellow lightning shoved the steers all up on their feet, milling around with eyes wildly rolling, fighting the small balls of red fire on the ends of their glistening horns. Their hair was soaked and stuck up every which way, and mud was splashed over their four quarters.

The men were stringing around them now. I saw old Ben Mitchell riding with his hat in his hand and the rain pouring down on his long gray hair and best britches. His hard-bitten face was lifted up at the storm and he was defying the powers that controlled it.

"Hit me, not the cattle!" he yelled, with plenty a cuss word in between. And when a closer crack came: "A little to the right, up there! Can't you see these here cattle?"

But most of the men were singing. I could hear them, one at a time, as they came close and rode past me, each chanting some little old tune that belonged to nobody but himself and made no sense to anybody else except the cattle. They seemed to understand it. Matt Thomas almost bumped into me, quavering far back in his throat. Sometimes there were words and sometimes just lonely sounds. If the river preacher had drunk three cups of whisky instead of coffee, this might have been what came out, half-church, half-saloon, and a little lobo and coyote up on the hill under a moon. But it was quieting the cattle.

They got the best of them now, I thought.

It had slacked up raining. Scarcely had I spoken to myself when it started coming down again in that sudden way it has on the plains when worse hangs over. I heard a crackle like great cedar logs burning and snapping. Then the bolt came. The sky cracked open and I could look straight into hell. One minute the steers were here and the next they were gone. It happened so quick you couldn't tell which was the lightning's thunder and which that of twenty or thirty thousand hoofs pounding the ground. The whole San Augustine plains rumbled and trembled.

There are things that can't be told. If you've ever been in a stampede or an avalanche, you know the feelings, and if you haven't, there are too few words to put them on paper. I could hear nothing now except thunder, but I knew that out there, although I couldn't see them, Doane and Tom Camber and all the rest were yelling and cursing and riding for all their horses had in them. My mount wanted to go, too, but I held him back. There was nothing I could do and little enough they could, but that wouldn't keep every man of them from staying with the herd, pounding hell for leather in that pitchy blackness, trying to find and turn the leaders, trusting to luck and their horses' night eyes to get them safely over draws and cut banks, dog holes and arroyos. A sudden, small and lonely figure in a vast blackness rent by yellow slits, I sat there in the rain while the herd got farther and farther away. Only God knew now how far those steers would run and endlessly scatter tonight.

A few men began to straggle back to the ranch house in the middle of next morning. They said the run had split the herd finer than kindling and each man had gathered and fetched in what he found when daylight came. The funny part, they said, was that Doane Williams had stuck all night with a bunch of TC steers, while those Tom Camber had driven in were mostly Box Bars.

It was all over then, I knew by my mother's face. She asked a guarded question or two to find if my father was all right. Then she said we'd go on home to the ranch. Before we got away, Doane came in on his borrowed Diamond D horse and saddle. His britches and shirt were plastered with dried mud. But his eyes still danced, and all he'd say about the run was that Booger Johnson had got thrown in a cactus patch.

"You know, Miz Farnham," he told, "when Booger came to, he claimed somebody'd nailed his vest to his back with ten-penny spikes."

Rudith was all for him now, and you could tell, by the quiet, pleasant look in his face, he was going to get his buggy ride with his girl at last.

Although my mother and I went around by Fugatt's to fetch Rudith's horse and sidesaddle home, she and Doane weren't back when we got there. It grew dark and still they didn't come in. About eight o'clock I heard a rig coming hell-bent, and it was they, with a strange, lathered buckskin on the side of the tongue where Midnight, the bob-tailed livery black, had been.

"You have any trouble?" my mother called, coming to the door with our bull's-eye lantern.

"Nothin' much," Doane answered.

"Nothing but having a rifle pulled down on us," Rudith

called back. Strangely enough, she had fine color in her cheeks and her eyes sparkled.

"It was just one of the TC boys we met on Cedar Ridge," Doane mentioned, helping Rudith carefully down between the buggy wheels. "His hoss had give out and, since we had two, I give him one. He said he'd leave him someplace for me."

"Couldn't a TC hand scare up a fresh mount for himself?"

"I don't expect he had much time." Doane started to unhitch one side while I took the other.

"A posse was after him?" my mother guessed sharply.

"Might be." Doane was mild as milk. "He didn't say, except he was in a hurry. Rue and me wasn't, so I rode out and roped us a buggy hoss to come home with."

"He doesn't look like a buggy horse to me," my mother said skeptically, walking around the rolling eyes of the lathered buckskin.

"I couldn't find one with collar marks," Doane mentioned.

My mother stopped. "You mean to tell me you broke in an outlaw on that narrow Cedar Ridge?"

"He's no outlaw, Miz Farnham," Doane soothed her. "A good saddle hoss, I judge. Of course, he pitched a little, since it was the first time he got hitched in a buggy. But he ran good on the end."

My mother just looked at him, and I could see the whole picture with her in her mind—the hitching up of the buckskin that never had harness on him before, his wild rebellion as soon as Doane let go of his head, the bucking, pitching and tangling up in the trace and pole there on that narrow trail on Cedar Ridge, the spurts of wild running with a two-hundred-foot drop into a canyon on either side, and all the while Doane sitting there beside Rudith, patient as could be, giving him plenty time to play his meanness out.

The Simple Life

My mother had the sourdough mixed when we came into the kitchen. She turned her strong face, with a helpless Southern look, to the door.

"You feel like making biscuits, Doane?"

"Why, sure, Miz Farnham," he said, going straight to the apron on the nail, tying it on and moving around the stove grave and easy. "I ain't done much all day and have nothin' on the string tomorrow."

No, he had only to drive the buggy tomorrow fifty-two miles back to the livery at Magdalena by daylight and then ride his horse forty-odd miles back to the roundup that night. He could sleep most of the way in the saddle. His mount knew the trail. The world was young and right side up. He had taken his girl home from the wedding and dance. As a matter of fact, we soon found out he had asked her to follow the lead of Billy and Kate, popping the question to her on that wild ride on Cedar Ridge to take her mind off the buckskin's pitching and the steep canyons below.

To travel, now, the wheel tracks Doane and Rudith took on their wild betrothal ride that day, you must get out and open some thirty gates and close them carefully behind you. And when you cross the paved highway you must watch out for roaring trucks that do in four hours what took poky old freighters a week. You must look out, too, for tourists and for young fellows speeding to town for a loaf of baker's bread or to take their girl to the picture show and dance. Oh, things move fast in the old West today. The tide of progress flows on and never ebbs. Times have changed, even on the range. Life out here is complex now. But back in the horse-and-buggy days, they say, life was very simple then.

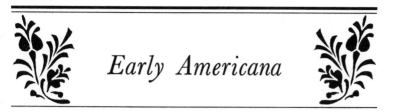

Early Americana

I T HAS SLIPPED ALMOST out of reality now, into the golden haze that covers Adobe Walls and the Alamo, so that today, behind speeding headlights or in the carpeted Pullman, it seems as if it might never have really been.

But if you are ever on the back of a horse at night far out on the wind-swept loneliness of the Staked Plains, with no light but the ancient horns of the Comanche moon and that milky band of stardust stirred up by the passing of some celestial herd, a cloud may darken the face of the un-tamed earth, the wind in your face will suddenly bring you the smell of cattle, and there beyond you for a moment on the dim, unfenced, roadless prairie you can make out a fabulous dark herd rolling, stretching, reaching majestically farther than the eye can see, grazing on the wild, unplanted mats of the buffalo grass.

And now with sudden emotion you know that the faint, twinkling light you see on the horizon is a distant window of that rude, vanished, half-mystical buffalo settle-ment, Carnuel, as it stood that night sixty-five years ago, the only fixed human habitation on a thousand square miles of unfriendly prairie, with great ricks of buffalo hides loom-ing up like bales of swarthy cotton on a Mississippi levee, and with John Minor standing silently on the gallery of his buffalo post, looking with unreadable eyes on the rude rutted trail running out of sight in the moonlight on its three hundred miles to the railroad, and thinking how many days it had been that no one, east or west, north or south, had come to Carnuel but the rugged old Kansas circuit rider for the settlement's first wedding.

As a rule, there were hide-buyers in hired buggies rattling in the protection of a wagon train coming back from Dodge; and across the prairie, hunters fresh from the big herds, yelling wildly as they rode up to Seery's saloon, the only place of refreshment in a dozen future counties; and clattering in from every direction, small freighters, their wagons piled high with hides, which lapped over the wheels to the ground so that they looked like huge hayricks bumping over the plain, swaying at every grass clump and threatening to crack the boom pole and spill the wagon. And at night the settlement would be full of bearded men stumbling over wagon tongues, roaring out lusty songs from Seery's bar, and in the smoky light of the post hefting the new rifles and buying cartridges and coffee.

But tonight the only sound from the gallery was the monotonous wind of the Staked Plains blowing soft and treacherous from the south, flapping the loose ends of five thousand buffalo hides, and bringing in from the prairie, now faint, now strong, the yelping of wolves from where cheery campfires of buffalo chips usually glowed.

In the adobe saloon, its walls marked with notorious names and ribald verses, Dan Seery and a single customer played euchre, the whisky-stained cards rattling on the drumlike hardness of a flint-dry buffalo-hide table.

In his little adobe house the bridegroom, Jack Shelby, took a last look at the room Nellie Hedd had put firmly in place for their wedding tomorrow, from the stove ready to be lighted by the bride's hand to the starched pillow shams on the bed, and then carefully stretched his own bed roll on the kitchen floor.

And in the living quarters behind John Minor's buffalo

post, Chatherine Minor, aged sixteen, tried not to listen to the voices of her father and the circuit rider coming low and grave from the storeroom as she brushed her black hair for bed by the light of a square buffalo-tallow candle, and thought of Laban Oldham, who had seldom spoken to her and never even looked at her, and wondered whether he might ask her for a square dance tomorrow night when they celebrated the wedding.

But ten miles out at Oldham Springs, in his father's dugout high and dry in the *cañada* bank, Laban Oldham wasn't thinking of Chatherine Minor. Straight and untalkative, for all his boyish cheeks, his eyes a deep crockery blue, the long rawhide-colored hair spilling violently over his linsey collar, he sat with his true love across his knees, polishing the octagon barrel, swabbing out the gleaming bore with bear oil, and rubbing the stock with tallow until it threw back a golden reflection of the candle.

For nearly four years he had done a man's work in the saddle. Tomorrow he would really be a man and his own boss at eighteen, and could go riding out of Carnuel, a buffalo hunter on the Staked Plains at last, leaving chores and drudgery forever behind him, his Sharps rifle hard in its scabbard under his leg, and his voice joining Frankie Murphy's in a kind of shouted and unrhymed singing:

> *I left my old wife in the county of Tyron.*
> *I'll never go back till they take me in irons.*
> *While I live, let me ride where the buffalo graze,*
> *When I die, set a bottle to the head of my grave.*

His mother, a small, dark woman, bent her face over her needle as if to blot the rifle from her eyes. His father, with a full, tawny mustache and a back like a bull, sat almost invisible in the shadows, silently smoking his pipe. And all evening there was no mention of missing freighters or buffalo hunters, or that it was the boy's last night in the dugout, only that the rotting tow sacks over the ceiling poles were letting the dirt sift through and that what they should do was go away for a night and leave the door open, so a polecat could come in and rid the place of mice.

"The wind's kind of bad from the south tonight," Jesse Oldham once remarked.

The others listened, but you couldn't hear the wind in a dugout.

"I stopped at the Hedds' today," Jesse Oldham spoke again. "Nellie sure looks pretty for her weddin'."

Another ten minutes passed while Jesse Oldham used the cottonwood bootjack and made himself ready for bed.

"You're staying in the settlement till after the wedding, Laban?" his mother begged him.

He nodded, but to himself he said that it was nothing to his liking. With his young eyes hard and pitying on Jack Shelby for giving in so weak to a woman, he would stand with the other men at the kitchen door and never go near the dancing. And at daybreak, when the celebration would be over and Jack Shelby would find himself tied for life to a house and a woman's corset strings, he and Frankie Murphy would be riding free as air out of Carnuel toward the Little Comanche, where the prairie was alive and moving with a dark tide, and where for ten miles you could hear the endless grunting bellows of fighting bulls, a dull, unceasing mutter that rose to an unforgettable thunder by dawn.

Something came into his blood at the thought, so that he could scarcely sit still. He could see himself and Frankie riding all spring and fall in the backwash of that shaggy tidal wave as it swept, eddied, and scattered over the far northern plains. They would sell their hides at Dodge and Hays City and perhaps Cheyenne. He would see strange tribes and people, the Arkansas River and the Platte, and the northern mountains that looked like blue clouds floating over the plain. It was a free life, a king's life, with always a new camp and a new country just over the rise. And at night, rolled snug with his companions in their blankets, with the moon sailing high or the snow falling softly, with roast buffalo hump keeping him warm and tomorrow another adventure, he knew he should never come back to sleep again in a house at Carnuel.

Long after the dugout was in darkness, he lay awake in his sagging pole bed, with the familiar scent of earthen walls and rye straw in his nostrils, feeling the warmth of his young brother under the blue quilt beside him and listening to his father and mother breathing in the red-cherry bed that had come in the wagons from Kentucky. His mother's breath was the faster. Rapidly it caught up to his father's deeper breathing, chimed with it, passed it, for all the world like the hoofbeats of Ben and Fanny, his father's and mother's saddle horses, on their way to Nellie Hedd's wedding tomorrow.

On his own speckled pony, Calico, he rode away in the morning, with no more fuss than Cass, his young brother, running admiringly beside him in the other wheel track, as if they were not going to see each other in a few hours at Carnuel. Perched on the bleached skull of a buffalo, the young boy waited until horse and rider were high on the rise against the sky.

"Good-by, Laban!" he shrilled.

Laban lifted his hand and rode down into his new world. If it hadn't been for Cass, he would have liked to turn his head for a last look at the place to carry with him into the country of the Cheyennes and the Sioux—the smoke lifting from his father's dugout, almost invisible within the bank; his mother's great black kettle, for which he had gathered wagonloads of buffalo chips; and swinging their long horns as they came in single file down over the cap rock, his father's red Texas cattle that had grazed the night with antelope and stray buffalo.

Down in the deep prairie crack along the Carnuel River, he passed the Hedd place, busy with preparation for the wedding, the bridegroom's saddled horse already tied to the cottonwood, the bride drying her dark red hair in the sunshine, and her father's pole buckboard waiting for horses by the door. And when he was up on the cap rock again, he could see rising behind the south ridge a cloud of dust that was surely a crowd of buffalo hunters riding in for Jack Shelby's wedding.

With his long, rawhide-colored hair leaping at every jump, he turned his pony southeast to meet them, but when he reached the top of the long grassy ridge, the dust had disappeared. And though he stayed there for hours, the wide plain below him remained empty of the crawling ants that would have numbered Frankie Murphy in his deerskin vest and Sam Thompson and Captain Jim Bailey bringing their wives home from their buffalo camps along the Little Comanche.

He had the strangest feeling when at last he turned his pony and rode slowly back to Carnuel. The tiny remote settlement lay in the westering sun like a handful of children's blocks thrown and forgotten on the immensity of the prairie. Still several miles away, he could see a small cluster of persons standing on the gallery of the post, but neither his parents' horses nor the Hedd buckboard had come up from the river.

When he reached the settlement, the spare form of the storekeeper moved out in the rutted trail to meet him.

"Nellie and Jack didn't get them a new day for their weddin'?" he asked in a low voice, but his gaze was sharp and piercing.

Early Americana

"Not when I passed there this mornin'." Out of the corner of one eye the boy glimpsed Chatherine Minor in a new maroon cashmere dress moving quietly to the side of her father. His hand tightened on his bridle rein. "I'll ride down and see what's keepin' them," he said briefly.

John Minor opened his leathery lips as if to say something, and closed them again, but the girl had stiffened.

"Don't go, Laban!" she cried after him.

He made as if he hadn't heard, sitting very straight in the saddle and not looking back, riding away at a steady lope on the familiar trail for the Hedd house and his father's dugout. He would have gone now if a norther had been blowing, white and blinding, across the prairie, but he had never seen the Staked Plains more gentle and mild. The wind had gone down and the late-afternoon sunlight slanting across the motionless grass was soft and golden as the candle burning in the little shrine on the wall of Mrs. Gonzales's house in Carnuel when her man, Florencio, was somewhere out in this desolate land.

Like a long shadow felled across his path, he reached the edge of the canyon and saw below him that his morning's trail of bright sunshine now lay in twilight and gloom. He pulled up his pony and listened. The rocky depths with their untamed fertile bottoms tangled with shanghai grass and willows, and even the river itself, were utterly silent. For a little he sat there looking back at Carnuel, that had somehow become a distant and golden speck on the sunlit prairie. Then he urged his pony down the trail that the indefatigable pick of Sebastian Hedd had cut wide enough for his buckboard in the sloping canyon wall.

It wasn't so bad, once he was down and accustomed to the heavy shadows, with Calico splashing cheerfully through the shallow river and the echo of iron shoes thrown back from the rocky walls. A little farther on, the canyon would be homelike, with Sebastian Hedd's fields green in this wild place with winter wheat, and beyond them the peeled logs of the Hedd cabin, with the buckboard drawn up to the door and Jack Shelby's horse tied under the cottonwod. Even Calico freshened and stepped briskly round the bend in the canyon wall.

It was there, as he expected—the house and the fields Sebastian Hedd had wrested from the wilds, and the old slatted buckboard standing in front of the house. And yet there was something wrong with the familiar scene, something that caused him slowly to stiffen and his pony to halt and snort in the gloomy trail. Jack Shelby's horse was curiously missing and the pole of the buckboard had been propped up on a boulder, and over it had been bent some peculiar and unfamiliar object, pale and glistening in the shadows, and utterly still.

With a fine, inexplicable sweat breaking out of his pores, the boy watched it, little by little edging his pony nearer and leaning over the saddle horn that he could better see. Then, as if struck by a rattlesnake, he stopped. He had made out a feathered shaft like a long, thin, uplifted finger warning him grimly not to come on. And now for the first time he knew the naked and mutilated object on the buckboard tongue for what it was.

A hundred times, night and day, sun and shadow, Laban had traveled this trail, but never had the walls of the canyon pushed in and choked him as they did today. He could feel the dark, open door of the wronged little house watching him. And far above him, the layers of cap rock still brilliant in the sun, were the bright walls of the holy city that he could never hope to reach again.

For endless minutes he sat there on Calico, his knees wedged against the pony's shoulders, rigid, waiting, twitching, listening. All he could hear was an unseen horned lark winging its way back to the cap rock from the river, uttering its nameless cry, that never betrayed the direction from which it came or whether it was bird or spirit. And all he could see were the contents of a bride's leather trunk, starched muslin underwear and petticoats, feather-stitched and trimmed with ruffles, and nightgowns high in the throat and tatted on the wrists, one of them given by his own mother, and all carefully folded away for the bridal journey, now torn and scattered like bits of white rubbish along the trail.

And now, examining again the loaded chamber of his old Sharps with the octagon barrel, he forced his rearing and plunging pony by the tragic little house, his eyes mechanically counting the three pitiable things lying motionless on buckboard tongue and ground.

Everywhere as he rode on rigidly through the canyon dusk, through the clumps of tangled willows that took on the shapes of bows and rifle barrels, and through the tall rank grass that twisted like snaky braids and eagle feathers, he could see his father more clearly than he had ever seen him in the life—splashing his face in the wash-tin before supper, wetting his hair, combing his long, tawny, imperturbable mustache, sitting without expression as he smoked in his chair after supper. And he could see his mother, her black hair combed tightly back from her forehead, tilting the huge coffeepot, carving a slice from the loaf, or riding sidewise on her man's saddle, her right knee hooked over the horn, and behind her his young brother holding on with both hands to the cantle and scratching his itching cheek against the rough homespun back of her basque.

Every fresh turn in the murky trail, boulders lying on the ground twisted the hand on his woolly rawhide reins, and up on the home side of the cap rock in the last searching rays of the sun, distant white specks in the grass flattened his cheeks until he knew them to be forgotten piles of bleaching buffalo bones. And when at last he reached the rise from where he had lifted a hand to Cass that morning, he could see below him in the grassy *cañada* the silent bank that was his father's dugout, and the door standing idly open on its wooden hinges.

Minute by minute he put off the grim duty, and when slowly he pushed his way into the doorway, he found the place as if a shell had struck it—the ticks ripped open, the floor littered with staves of his mother's sourdough keg, and broken pieces of the beautifully polished red-cherry bed that had come all the way from Kentucky in the wagons, and flour and savage filth over everything. The buffalo robe where Cass used to lie of an evening on the floor before the earthen fireplace was gone without a trace, and so were Cass and his father and mother, the hoofprints of the unshod Ben and Fanny lost among the endless trample of unshod ponies.

Long after darkness had fallen, the boy half-ran beside his grunting pony climbing out of the deep silent canyon. Up here on the cap rock he could breathe again. The stars seemed only half as far away. And far across the blackness of the plains he could see that reassuring small spark of yellow light, steady, alive, and more beautiful than all the stars in the sky.

He told himself that his father, who knew the country better than an almanac, might have left his mother in the soft radiance of that light at this moment. And when he rode up in front of the lighted post, the first thing he did was to peer from the saddle toward the dusty panes. But all he could see was the candlelight shining on brand-new cinches and cartridge belts and skillets strung along the rafters and on the full skirts of three women, none of whom was his small mother with her black hair combed tightly back from her forehead.

"That you, Labe?" the voice of the storekeeper came from the dimness.

The boy moved his pony back deeper into the shadows.

"Could you come out here, Mr. Minor?" he said in a low tone. "The women, I reckon, better stay where they're at."

At the peculiar quality in his voice, four men, two with rifles, moved with silent stiffness from where they had been standing unseen on the dark side of the gallery—the storekeeper and the saloonkeeper, the gaunt circuit rider, and Seth Falk, a buffalo hunter from Indian territory, thick, bearded, in a buckskin shirt and an old pied brown and white calfskin vest.

"What's the matter, boy?" the circuit rider demanded.

Laban only looked at him, his eyes burning like coals in the darkness.

"I reckon," after a moment he told them, "there won't be a weddin' in the settlement now."

Silence followed, except for the short, rapid puffs of Dan Seery's pipe and the circuit rider's hard breathing. Only Seth Falk changed no more than an Indian.

Laban could see him standing there in the dim light, leaning on his rifle, taciturn, inscrutable, his heavy forehead bent characteristically forward. His unreadable black eyes watched the boy from under the edge of his twisted hat-brim.

"They get Jack and the girl both?" he questioned without emotion.

"They got them all," the boy said thickly.

"How about your folks?" John Minor wanted to know.

Laban told him. And when he spoke again, it was very low, so the girl, who, he knew, was standing at the open door of the post, couldn't hear him.

"I got Nellie here on Calico now. She's wrapped up in my sugan." He made every effort to keep his voice from breaking. "You better tell the women not to open it. They did her up mighty bad."

The circuit rider, who was standing nearest the dim shadow of the pony, stiffened as if touched by a grisly hand, and Dan Seery's eyes rolled white. But Seth Falk and John Minor did not move.

For a time the four of them stood staring at him and out into the night and at each other and through the open door of the post to the untold women, while a stark awareness grew on the boy that not a wolf or coyote howled on the cap rock this evening.

"We better get Jack and Bass tonight—if we want to bury them," he said bleakly.

"I'll ride down with the boy," Seth Falk spat, and moved off toward the rock corral with his rifle, for all his size as light on his feet as a mountain cat in the darkness.

The Comanche moon hung low in the west as the two horses came slowly and heavily back across the plain from the canyon. In the shadow of the post John Minor and the circuit rider stood waist deep in a wide, sandy trench. There were no boards to waste on a coffin. The three women came slowly out of the post, and the circuit rider put on his long, dark coat to read the burial service. A tall, gaunt, unforgettable figure in rusty black, towering there in front of a pile of shaggy buffalo hides, his voice rang out into the night as if to reach and sear the red infidels where he pictured them lying on the ground like wolves and harlots with their sinful and bloody scalps.

Laban had bared his long, sandy hair at a burial before, but never one that constricted him like this—the late hour, the small handful of people, the rising and falling of a real preacher's voice making the hair on the back of his neck to stir, and all the time the grated tin lantern with its tiny pane of glass and scattered air-holes throwing grotesque shadows

on the men with rifles, on the full skirts of the women, still
dressed for the wedding, and on the house of Jack Shelby,
empty and silent yonder in the darkness.

Even here, when she stood only a few feet from him,
the boy did not glance at the tight-lipped face of Chatherine
Minor. A blur of maroon dress was all he saw or cared to
see. White women didn't belong out here. Their place was
back in a gentler land where farmers never heard of turning a furrow with a rifle lashed to the plow handles and
where, on a Sunday morning, his mother used to say, she
could still remember the peaceful sound of church bells
drifting across the blue-grass. And tonight, if they had
stayed there, no girl with luxuriant dark-red hair would be
lying out here to be buried without it in an old mended sugan
for a coffin, and his mother might be surely alive and rocking on a board floor in a Kentucky town with a lighted lamp-
post on the corner.

" 'The Lord giveth,' " the circuit rider declared, " 'and the
Lord taketh away. And no man knoweth the hour at which
the Son of Man cometh.' "

As if in pagan challenge to the Christian words, a sign
appeared slowly out in the darkness, then another. And
presently, as they stood there watching, with the lips of Mrs.
Gonzales moving in Spanish and her hand convulsively
crossing the black shawl folded on her breast, three fires far
out on the plain burned red holes into the night, a scarlet
triangle around the little settlement, fading and flaring in
some savage code.

" 'And I stood upon the sand of the sea,' " the circuit
rider said, with abomination in his voice, " 'and saw a beast
rise up out of the sea, having seven heads and ten horns.' "

Sternly, when the rude service was done, John Minor
ordered the women into the post, and for a time there was
only the whisper of falling sand.

"What are they sayin', Falky?" Dan Seery asked.

"I ain't sartain I savvy," the buffalo hunter muttered. But Laban observed that he gave John Minor a meaning look and then stood with his head thrown forward grimly, watching the fires wax and wane.

For long minutes while they burned to smoldering red sparks on the prairie, John Minor mechanically mounded the wide grave with his shovel, his face bleak and marked, as if what he thought lay too deep in his mind to fetch up without herculean effort.

"There's something I want to say to you, men," he said at last unsparingly.

The boy had been watching his face. He wasn't sure what the storekeeper was about to say, but whatever it was, he was with him. Only the buffalo hunter seemed to know. He swung around slowly. All evening he had said little, and he said nothing now, but his eyes were like burning black fragments as they threw a deep, unutterable look around the little circle, not as if searching their faces, but from some powerful, unspoken feeling.

"I've no notion," John Minor went on harshly, "of letting our women go through what Nellie Hedd went through before those devils scalped her."

Laban felt a sharp, prophetic stab of coldness, as if slivers of blood had congealed in his veins. But John Minor had picked up an old buffalo horn and was bent over his shovel, scraping off the blade with all the deliberation of a man who expected to use it for a long time to come.

"What's this you're talking about, man?" the circuit rider demanded sharply.

"The women." John Minor didn't look up at him. "Three of us got to keep extra guns loaded. We'll hold out as long as we can. Then, if it has to be, it's an act of mercy."

He said no more, but Laban felt strangely weak in the

knees. Dan Seery's eyes were white and glistening in his beard, and for a moment even the rugged face of the circuit rider lost some of its color. Only Seth Falk stood there stony and unchanged. And presently he brought out a deck of worn Mexican cards that fetched the quick censure into the circuit rider's cheeks.

"I've throwed out the queen of clubs," he told John Minor.

"I reckon that's good as any other way," the storekeeper said. "Who must we say for the queen of spades? Mrs. Gonzales. And Sadie Harrison for the queen of diamonds. And the queen of hearts"—for a moment his face was like leather strained over a drum—"will have to be the other one." He turned and started to pull down a hide that had worked loose from the pile.

"You all savvy?" Seth Falk's gaze swept the men.

With its grotesque legs and clotted ruff, the hide lay on the ground like some dark misshapen omen, scarred and bloodstained, its swarthy wool matted with ticks and sand-burs, bearing the tin lantern and the pack of cards face downward beside it.

"You draw fust, Dan," the buffalo hunter said briefly.

The saloonkeeper made no movement—just stood there looking down at the deck as if paralyzed. John Minor knelt and lifted a card. When Laban saw them glance expectantly at him, he stiffened his back and drew the second. It was the four of spades. The buffalo hunter followed. Relentlessly now, the drawing went on. With strong disapproval on his face, the circuit rider moved away, and came back again in his long black coat to watch like a gigantic dark moth drawn to the flame.

It seemed to the rigid boy that, except for the slight hiss of the slipping cards, the Staked Plains had never been so hushed. The horned moon had set. The fresh grave slept peacefully. Not a sound came from the post. Their little circle of light lay on the ground like a golden coin in all this illimitable darkness which somewhere held his father and mother and little Cass.

He was dimly aware of turning up a card with a broken corner which suddenly froze in his hands. It was a woman riding a horse, as the queen does in the Mexican deck, her colored raiment stained and blemished, her face almost obliterated, and above the horse's head the small, curious-shaped Mexican heart. And as soon as he laid it down on the swarthy hide, it turned into the slender body of Chatherine Minor lying silent on the dark adobe floor of the post in the full skirts of the maroon cashmere dress she had made for Nellie Hedd's wedding.

He remembered afterward John Minor's granite face, and Seth Falk tossing down the queen of yellow diamonds with no more expression than a card in a poker hand, and the latter's little black buffalo eyes watching him as if his face bore some unbecoming color.

"Come in and John'll give you a drink," he said gruffly.

Laban stood there, rude and unhearing. When the others had gone with the lantern into the post, he kept walking with his rifle between the dark piles of hides.

The strong reek of the skins gave him something that he needed, like a powerful medicine brewed from the Staked Plains themselves. It reached where no whisky could. Kiowas or Comanches were nothing. After what he had seen in the canyon this afternoon, he could mow the painted devils down all day and stay icy cold with hate and clear of regret. But a white person, a woman, and only a girl! For more than an hour he kept walking up and down between the dark piles, and all the while, in the tightened sinews of his arms and legs and in the growing flatness of his cheeks, he seemed to be curing, hardening, drying, almost like one of the buffalo hides itself.

Early Americana

It was very quiet in the post when he came in. Over in a corner, so deep in shadows it seemed impossible to distinguish the faces of the cards, Seth Falk was playing a stolid game of solitaire on a boot-box, a pair of rifles lying beside him on the floor. Sitting under a candle, his Bible open on his knees, was the circuit rider, his rugged face alight as if the sun were shining into some rocky canyon. Dan Seery had just poured himself a stiff drink in a tumbler from a jug beneath the counter. And John Minor, with two guns leaning against the wall, sat writing slowly and methodically at his littered table.

He glanced up as Laban came in and silently indicated an extra rifle lying across a sugar barrel, with several boxes of cartridges on the floor. Something unutterable passed through the boy as he saw it, but he walked over, lifted and sighted it in his cold hands, the newest in buffalo guns, with a coil-spring lever and a long, round barrel. His stiff fingers tried a cartridge in the chamber, then they filled the magazine.

And now he knew that nothing could keep him from looking at the women. They had refused to go to bed, and there they sat in the two high-backed chimney seats. The Mexican woman, Mrs. Gonzales, was asleep, her chin forward on her breast, breathing into her tightly drawn *rebozo*. Beside her, the elderly Sadie Harrison's eyes were tightly closed in their bony sockets, her gray hair awry, her long face a picture of aged and bitter resignation.

Only the girl Chatherine was erect and awake, sitting alone on the other bench, her back toward him, hidden behind a post, except for one shoulder and for her full red skirts flowing over the side of the bench to the floor. Once he felt that she was about to turn her head and glance back at him, and he dropped his eyes and began pushing cartridges from the new boxes into the empty loops of his belt.

The clock struck, and the long silence that followed

rang louder than the gong. It was this waiting, waiting, Laban told himself, that was going to tell on him. He saw that the circuit rider had closed his Bible and was holding it tightly, like some golden talisman that would warm his cold hands. Seth Falk had shoved up the rows of his unfinished game and was stacking the cards on the box. Leaving one of his rifles against the doorjamb, he stepped outside, and Laban could hear his boots clicking no more loudly than a cat's claws up and down the adobe floor of the dark side of the gallery.

John Minor picked up one of his own rifles and started toward the kitchen.

"I'll watch it out there, Mr. Minor," Laban said quickly.

He was glad to get out of this place, where, no matter which way he turned his head, he could feel a red woolen dress burning into his eyes. He stepped through the darkened kitchen and out of the kitchen door. Not a star shone in the blackness. No sound rose but the faint stamping of horses around to the front, where they had been tied for the night to the gallery posts.

Once he heard the clock strike the half-hour and afterward the rumbling of a moved bench in the post, and then the circuit rider's unmistakable ecclesiastical voice. It seemed to go on and on, and when Laban pushed in the kitchen door, it rang suddenly louder. Curiously he made his way in the dimness to the other door. The candles in the post had burned out and only a pale rosy glow from the dying embers in the fireplace faintly illumined the long, spectral room. In a little circle of shadows, everyone seemed to be standing, the gaunt shadow that was the circuit rider towering above them all, something upheld in one hand, the other dipping into it like the mysterious hand of God. And his voice rang out with powerful solemnity in this unaccustomed place.

"I baptize thee . . . Chatherine Lydia Minor . . . in the

name of the Father . . . and the Son . . . and the Holy Ghost."

Slowly the meaning of the baptism tonight came over the boy, and with his fingers biting deeply into his rifle, he slipped back to a kitchen bench. But all the time he grimly sat there he had the feeling that even in that faintest of fantastic light Chatherine Minor had marked his tall form standing and watching at the kitchen door. And when it was all over, he heard her step coming toward him in the kitchen and then her fingers lighting the stub of a candle on the table.

"Can I make some coffee for you, Laban?" she asked.

And now he knew that nothing on earth could keep him from raising his eyes and letting them fall rigidly and for the first time directly on this girl whom, before the sun was an hour high, he might have to turn suddenly and bleakly upon.

There she stood, her dark eyes calmly facing him, taller than he imagined, but already, at sixteen, a woman, her body sturdy as a young cedar in the river brakes. The strong cheekbones in her face turned abruptly inward, giving a re-solute cast to the mouth. But what held his eyes most was her long, black hair, parted in a clear white streak, lustrous hair that, he knew, a Kiowa or Comanche would sell his life for.

He shook his head. She did not go away abashed; only stood there looking at him.

"You look thin, Laban," she reproved him. "You haven't had anything to eat since this morning."

He could see now that her eyes were not black and brazen, as he had thought. They were steady and slaty gray. But what made him steel himself, sitting there with a rifle across his lap, was where her left breast, swelling gently in the folds of her tight red basque, marked the target of her heart.

127

"I'm not hungry," he said harshly.

She turned quietly away, and he thought she would go, but he could hear her hand on stove and water bucket and kitchen utensils, and the heel of her firm foot on the adobe floor, and finally there was the fragrance of coffee through the kitchen, almost choking him, and he tried not to look at the picture she made, straight and with a disturbing womanly serenity, handing him a heavy, steaming, white cup and saucer and then bearing one in each hand into the post.

She set a plate of cold roast buffalo hump on the bench beside him and quietly washed the cups and saucers in the wash-tin and put them away on the calico-hung shelves as if she would surely find them there in the morning. Then her competent hands filled the stove, and with a dour mouth he watched her throw her skirts forward to seat herself, sturdy and erect, on the other kitchen bench.

"Papa wants me to stay out here," she said quietly, as if it were the most common thing in the world.

He said nothing. His face, framed in his long, rawhide-colored hair, was deaf and wintry. He waited grimly for her woman's chitchat, but she sat composed and silent as a man while the stub of a candle flickered out behind them, leaving the scent of burned wicking floating through the dark room.

For a long time they sat in utter silence while the clock struck and a faint gray began to drift like some thin, ghostly semblance of light through the dark window.

"It's starting to get morning, Laban," she whispered. "Are you awake?"

"I'm awake," he told her.

"I think I hear something," she said quietly.

His hands made sure of his rifles. Rising, he felt his way along the cool wall to where an iron bar, fashioned from an old wagon tire, bolted the door. Minutes passed while he stood there listening, and the black eastern sky grew into a long, lonely stretch of gray, unbroken except for a single well of green that lay like a pool reflecting the evening on a dark lava plain. He had never heard it more preternaturally still. The post at their backs was like the grave. Even the stamping horses were still. He could fancy them in his mind, standing out there in the early light, curving their necks to snuff and listen.

"It isn't anything," he told her. "Just the blood in your ears."

But now that he would deny it, he could hear it for the first time himself, very far away, like the wind in the grass, or the distant Carnuel River rushing down its canyon after a rain, nearer, always faintly nearer, and then evaporating into nothing more than the vast sweep of dark gray sky torn with ragged fissures like the chaos of creation morning.

"It wasn't anything," the girl agreed, whispering. "Just the blood in my ears."

But Laban's fingers were tightening again on the eight-sided barrel of his old Sharps. Something was surely out there, hidden from the post in the mists, like the abandoned hide wagons bleaching their bones on the Staked Plains. And now, far out on the prairie, he could see them breaking out of the fog rolling in from the river, a thin line of loping riders, the long-awaited crawling ants his eyes had strained for from the ridge that day so long ago that was only yesterday afternoon.

A bench was suddenly overturned in the post. Seth Falk's iron gray nickered. And now they could hear the pleasantest sound in more than a week—the distant hallooing of rough, stentorian voices. And presently the post was filled with bearded men twenty-four hours overdue for Nellie Hedd's wedding, men who had ridden all night in wet checkered linsey shirts and soaked blue flannel shirts and steaming buckskin shirts that smelled of countless hides and buffalo-chip campfires and black powder and Staked Plains rain. And all morning the thick tobacco smoke in the post drifted to the grave talk over Jack Shelby and the Hedds and the uprising of the Kiowas, who meant to sweep every white hunter from the buffalo country, and the lost hides, wagons and hair of the men who had waited too long before raising dust for the big outfits corralled together on the Little Comanche.

For two days and nights Laban Oldham sat cross-legged or lay in his blankets beside the campfire of Frankie Murphy's men. But all the time while he heard how his mother had ridden into a buffalo camp with her black hair streaming into little Cass's face, and while he listened for the long train of freighters coming with the women and hides, Laban couldn't feel anything half so clearly as Chatherine Minor's snug, warm kitchen, and Chatherine Minor handing him a cup of coffee, with the steam curling over her raven hair, and Chatherine Minor sitting up with him most of the night in the darkened kitchen and whispering to him in the morning if he were awake.

Tall and stiff, the third evening, his long, rawhide-colored hair gravely swinging, he walked through the post into the now familiar kitchen doorway and beyond, where a girl with her sleeves rolled high stood stirring sourdough leaven into flour that was not so white as her arms. She did not look around at his step, but her bare upper arms brushed, with quick womanly gestures, stray hairs from her face.

"It's a warm evenin'," he greeted.

"Good evening, Laban." She bent over her work, and her hands made the mixing-pan sing on the table.

"Did you hear the freighters are campin' tonight at

Antelope Water?" he went on awkwardly. "Bob Hollister just rode in."

"I reckon you'll be glad to see your folks," she answered, but he thought her deft white hands kneaded more slowly after that.

He sat on the familiar bench and waited unhurriedly for her to be through. The kitchen felt snug and pleasant as the dugout at home—the blur of the red-checkered cloth folded back from the table and the sputter of river cottonwood in the stove and the homely scent of the sourdough crock. He could close his eyes and know that either his mother or Chatherine Minor must be here. And when the tins were set to rise on the lid of the red flour-bin, she washed her hands and seated herself on the other bench, throwing her full skirts skillfully forward, as she had that sterner evening a day or two ago, until they rustled into their rightful place.

For a long time they sat there looking at the wall, that held no rifles now, and at the harmless black window, and at each other. And he told himself that he had never thought she would be a woman like this, with her flesh white as snow where it came out of the homespun at her throat, and the soft strength of her young mouth.

"I'm followin' the herd north when it moves, Chatherine," he stammered at length. "But I'm comin' back."

She answered nothing to that.

"I reckoned," he went on rigidly, "maybe you'd wait for me till I got back?"

She looked at him now, and her glance was firm and steady as the prairie itself. "I couldn't promise to wait for a single man, Laban," she said. "Where you're going is a long ways off. And a buffalo hunter can easy forget the way back."

The warm color stung his cheeks at that, and he stood

on his feet very tall, and stepped across the floor and sat down on the bench, and laid his linsey-clad arm rudely around her shoulders.

"The circuit rider isn't gone back to Dodge with the freighters yet," he reminded. "You can make it that he didn't come to Carnuel for nothin', if you want to, Chatherine. Then you won't have to do your waitin' for a single man."

She didn't say anything, but neither did she shake him off, and they sat quiet again while the talk in the post receded to a mere faraway drone and the kitchen candle burned out again, leaving its fragrance and all the room in darkness, except where a dim rectangle of post light fell across the floor. And suddenly he noticed that her breath caught up to his, chimed with it, and passed it, for all the world like the breathing of his father and mother in the beautiful red-cherry bed that had come from Kentucky in the wagons.

And everything, he thought, was well, when of a sudden she buried her face in his shirt and cried, and what she said after that, he thought, was very strange.

"Oh, Laban," her voice came muffled, "she had such beautiful hair!"

Before the week was out, the circuit rider scratched out the names of John McAllister Shelby and Nellie Hedd from an official paper and firmly wrote: "Laban Oldham and Chatherine Lydia Minor." And the settlement had its wedding with four women on the pole-backed chimney seats, and with Mrs. Oldham, her dark hair combed back tightly from her forehead, sitting on the chair of honor, and with Jesse Oldham, his back like a bull and his imperturbable mustache, standing with John Minor, and with buffalo hunters along the counter, and the freighters in a reticent knot by the door.

The circuit rider's voice rang in the pans and skillets

hanging on the smoke-stained rafters. And when it was over, a huge shaggy hunter rode his horse halfway into the post's open doorway and bellowed for Dan Seery to unlock the saloon. And when he saw the silent couple and the black book of the circuit rider, he stood in his stirrups and roared, shaking his long, gray mane and the bloodstained, weather-beaten fringe of his buckskins till he looked, like an old buffalo bull coming out of the wallow:

> *I left my old wife in the county of Tyron.*
> *I'll never go back till they take me in irons.*
> *While I live, let me ride where the buffalo graze.*
> *When I die, set a bottle to the head of my grave.*

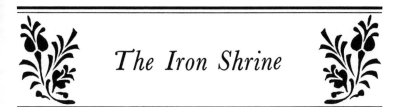

The Iron Shrine

THE OLD MAN IN the big house heard the carriage stop and the sound of men's voices. He guessed what they wanted. Let them come, he said to himself, and his lip twitched in sardonic humor. Others had come before them, and none had got the secret out of him yet. But they'd better move fast. Wasn't he supposed to be on his deathbed? Any day now his mind might not be clear or he might be gone to that bourn from which no man returneth, or so the parson on his visits to cheer the sick had told him.

Well, it was true he was old and had taken to his bed. But he wasn't laid out yet, not by a long shot. He wasn't even upstairs. He'd ordered his housekeeper, the cook, and the yard man to fetch his bed down. He told them it would save them running upstairs with trays and downstairs with slops, but all the time he and they knew the real reason. He didn't want to give up being among the living. He didn't want to leave this corner room on the first floor he called his office. Most of his life had been spent here with his high desk and stool, his low desk table and chair with the familiar worn red cushion. Here were his shelves of furnace accounts and records, on the wall a row of wooden pegs with his clothes, including his blue Army overcoat, his cocked hat and sword.

Upstairs, the green clutter of leaves shut out everything. Down here he could look out and see his furnace against the hill, built of the same gray-brown stone as the house, everything still intact outside and in, even the ore barrows and charcoal wagons on the upper level. The stack needed only ore, limestone and charcoal to be fired. But the brown-painted shutters on the furnace were closed tight and the experienced eye saw no heat waves rising against the sky.

He could hear the men now entering the iron gate to the grounds. They would lower their voices presently. The house always sobered people when they got close—the huge, solid bulk of it, the tiers of white shutters against the mountain stone, the large windows with their small panes, the big front door with the carved window light above, and the long lights on either hand. The furnace men used to say that if the sidelights would swing with the door, you could drive a team through.

The bell on its long rope tinkled. Presently the old man could hear Manda moving through the house to answer it. His lips pursed in ironic anticipation. They were curious lips seen sometimes on the Scotch; not exactly thick, but ropy, as if they got in the way, and he had them always to contend with. Ansell Sloan had white hair above, while a ring of the same ran below from his ears like a thin strip of hairy hide pasted around his bare chin. In this frame his face looked like that of a crabbed but lovable saint, so that you forgot the uncompromising lips and wondered how a man with such a gentle, wry face could have had the nickname of Iron Sloan as a soldier before he became an ironmaster.

You could see the strangers relax when they saw him. The house and grounds might be formidable, but this old man would be easy to handle. He didn't look like an iron soldier to them. They were shrewd, sharp-eyed men from Uniontown, with fine clothes and well-fed faces. First they complimented him on the house and grounds. Then they asked about the two paintings.

"This one toward the road was my wife," he said. "The other one, with the flowers under it, was my mother-in-law."

"Isn't that a little unusual, General?" one of them asked, smiling. "Flowers for your mother-in-law?"

"Not for Mary Harris," the old man said, quickly. "But that's a long story."

They didn't press him. They were interested in something else, something more valuable than a mother-in-law.

"We understand, General, that not all your iron came from the Cornwall mines." The leader of the group got down to business. "You told some people, I believe, that the best quality iron you ever had came from a secret source of your own."

"Ah!" The ironmaster rubbed a stubbly chin. "So you heard this even as far as Uniontown?"

"It's true then, General, that you owed your success to a secret iron mine?"

"Well, yes, I guess it's true, though I wouldn't call it an iron mine. It's just where my best iron came from. But remember now I didn't say where I got it."

The men licked their lips and hitched closer. "Was this source pretty far away? Did it cost you much to freight it here?"

"Didn't cost me hardly nothing."

"You say it was very rich iron?"

"About the best I ever knew."

"Was it worked out?"

"God bless you, no. It gave iron to some others who knew about it, and still does to me when I need it."

You could see victory now on their faces. "Will you, for a consideration, General, draw us a map of the location?"

"No, I couldn't do that."

There was consternation on their faces. "Why not?"

"Because I don't think you could find it."

"That would be our risk. This iron is still in existence?"

"Well, yes, some of it. But the source has moved."

"Moved? How could it move? You said it was never worked out."

"That's true," he agreed.

He could see with enjoyment that they were completely baffled, that they thought him a queer old man. Well, maybe he was. You got queer sometimes in your eighties. Not that they gave up easily. For more than an hour they pestered and cross-examined him. In the end, like the others, they had to go without it, saying they would be back again.

He sat chuckling dryly when they had left. So they wanted to buy his iron mine? Well, they weren't the first, and likely wouldn't be the last. But never would he tell them. They wouldn't believe it had been a woman. They wouldn't understand what he was talking about. You had to live back in the 1750's to understand. Today, in the Millburn Valley, you saw mostly fields of grain and corn, with plenty of cattle, grass, fat barns and peaceful farmhouses. But then all was solid woods and swamps with thick vines running up the big butts in the bottoms, with cabins buried in the wild greenness, with alarms from the savages twice a year and waking up some morning to find your neighbors killed and their cabins burned. You might even wake up and find it done to your own folks.

———————————

THAT'S WHAT HAD HAPPENED TO HIM, and him only eight years old. When he fought back and cried, one of the savages gave him a blow, and he remembered nothing till they shook him and threw water on him to get him going. For a week after that, it seemed, they dragged him through the forest, first a large party, then just two, tying him to one or the other of them, jerking him through bogs and runs, driving him over logs and roots. Hardly was he alive when they reached the other Indian party, waiting for them with a captive at a hemlock spring.

Never as long as he lived would he forget the sight of this unknown spot in the wilderness, with the black mountain above, the painted savage faces around the fire below, the ghastly flutter of scalps on stretchers, and sitting on the ground nearby the young white captive, Mary Harris, with her baby at her breast. She wore a gray homespun short gown, muddied and torn by the bush. Her hair was black, her face brown. She was barefoot and her legs badly scratched by roots and briers. Her state looked hopeless, and yet the way she sat there, living for herself, paying no attention to her captors or her fate, gave him the first sensation of life and hope since he was taken. He tried to run to her, but the Indian he was tied to jerked him and he fell to the ground.

He got to his feet, shaken and trembling. Had she sympathized with him a lick by word or look, his tears would have turned into a flood.

"Don't mind them; they don't know no better," she said matter-of-factly.

"They killed my ma and pa!" he cried.

She made resigned noises with her tongue, like a grandmother. "Maybe your ma and pa are lucky. They don't need to go through what me and you do."

"I wish they'd 'a' killed me too."

"Oh, no, you don't," she said dully, almost flatly. "They broke in a young boy's head for cryin' a ways back. You don't wish you was him a-lyin' back there with his brains on a tree."

What she said sickened him. He pitied himself. To show how bad he felt, he made himself cry noisily. To his surprise, she turned her head away. He bawled and cried, but she acted as if she didn't know he was there. He called out the most pitiful things to make her feel sorry for him, so he could cry with more reason, but she might have been stone-deaf for all the notice of it she took. He found his eyes drying up despite himself. Though he tried to fetch tears again, none would come. Bitterness and hate for her rose in him instead.

"Don't you know me? I'm Ansell Sloan! They call me Andy in Black Run!" he cried at her.

He might as well have been crying to the wind. She sat calm and contained, attending her baby. That puny thing and herself were all that mattered to her. She was like an Indian herself, and next day when they moved through the woods, he watched her carry her pack of savage booty like a squaw. Not once did he hear her rebel or complain. He was only a boy, but twice with spirit he threw off the stolen horns heavy with powder they had hung around his neck. In the end, he had to carry them anyhow, along with the cuts and bruises they gave him.

Now wouldn't you reckon she'd feel for him when his captors beat him so that he would sob for a long time afterward? But hardly a word from her, except to taunt him for bawling. Then hate for her would make him stop quick enough. No sooner would they camp in the evening and the fire at dusk set him crying for home than she would mock him for it until he answered in kind.

The Indians only laughed and egged them on. This was a big joke to them, something that gave the savages pleasure —two white persons who couldn't stand together against their common enemy, but fought each other. Most always after a fight between them, the Indians treated her better and slackened her bonds.

"Injun pet! Turncoat!" He scorned her more than once, but she gave him no notice that she had heard.

For days the party marched through the woods. Once they stopped while two of their men stole away to bring back mysterious news in their own language. Next morning the party split, and the captives were left in camp under the guard of a savage they called Onchedunk. Andy cried when the Indian tied him so tight that it hurt.

The Iron Shrine

"Watch out. Don't cross him," Mary Harris warned. "He's the one that massacreed the other boy."

"You care more about that other boy than me!" Andy accused.

"I ought to," Mary Harris said bitterly. "He was my own Billy."

Andy looked at her with a sudden start. He was sober now. His eyes went dry. He stared uneasily at the savage who had done it, his face painted in colors that had run in the rain so that they distorted his features. A large bunch of hair from some former scalping had been dyed bright red and fixed to the top of his head, while a piece of bright metal hung from his nose and covered much of his mouth, so that he looked like a picture of the devil.

Now how could Mary Harris let such a terrifying creature hurt her and never whimper? He trussed her so that hardly could she hold her babe. He pulled on the knots so it must have cut into her woman's flesh. And all the time he was the one who had killed and scalped her own boy before her eyes. And yet her face hardly changed. Not a complaint did she make. Then Onchedunk took his gun and left.

It wasn't long afterward when a flock of migrating birds, mostly with red-speckled breasts, swarmed into camp, picking up crumbs from around the fire. They must have taken the two bound prisoners for stumps, for they flittered close to both, and especially the young woman, chittering and chirping until finally they flew off into the woods.

"Them birds say anything to you?" Mary Harris asked, when they had gone.

"Birds can't talk," the boy told her.

"Oh, they don't talk sniveling and pigeon-hearted like you," she said. "Their talk was spunky and cheerful. They said, What was I doin' here? Why didn't I up and go?"

The boy looked at Mary Harris strangely. He had heard that being captured by Indians sometimes affected white

141

minds. Now he saw her begin to inch herself and child toward the fire. When she got there, she struggled to hold her bound bare legs over the low flame. The boy watched. He saw the white ankles grow black with burn, but still she kept them there. Several times her legs tried to burst the bonds, but she had to put herself again to the fire. In the end, the rawhide snapped, but not until a long, painful time had passed. Then she moved quickly to the pile of booty. With her bare toes she pulled out a rusty ax taken from some ravaged white cabin. Holding the blade up between her feet, she bent forward and severed the thongs binding her arms.

Now wasn't it a shame that this was when Onchedunk chose to return. They heard him coming. She tried to get back where she had been, putting the broken strips of hide around her, but before she was settled, he was there. Never in his life would the boy forget the look on the returned Indian's face—a look of fierce rage that she had tried to escape. With the barrel of his gun, he gave her a blow that knocked her over on the ground.

The baby screamed.

"Give um!" Onchedunk said, dropping his gun and holding out his hands for the child.

When she refused, he tore at the baby with both hands. Then she let it go sooner than see its tiny arms pulled from their sockets. Twisting his face, Onchedunk lifted it up to dash the small head against a tree. At the sight, Mary Harris sprang like a she panther. She snatched up the rusty ax and went for him. The Indian saw her coming and quickly laid down the screaming child, motioning for her to do the same with the ax.

"No, you wily snake in the grass!" she answered, and the boy had never seen her eyes so black. "You'd murder us both!"

The Iron Shrine

It was doubtful if the savage understood the words, but he did her face and manner. Jerking at the hatchet in his belt with one hand, he reached for his gun with the other. Before he got hold of it, she was on him with her weapon.

"Now it's either you or us!" she cried.

The boy shut his eyes. He heard a confused series of sounds, but except for the screaming of the baby, he couldn't tell what they were. In his heart he believed that no half-starved, barefooted white woman, not even an outraged mother, could be a match for this Indian. The crying of the baby suddenly ceased. He shuddered, closing his eyes the tighter, waiting for his own end.

"You can look now. It's all over," he heard Mary Harris say. When he opened his eyes, the Indian lay on his face, and the baby was back in the arms of its mother.

"Did you kill him?" he stammered.

"He'd 'a' took our hair, but we won't take his," she said.

"He looks so—bloody," Andy whimpered.

"How do you expect him to look?" she demanded. "You want your enemies done away with before they do away with you, but you want somebody else to do it someplace where you can't see it. Well, sometimes God Almighty puts you in a place where you got to do it your own self as best you can."

It took only a few moments to cut his thongs.

"I don't know whether to leave you or take you along," she said. "They'll likely kill you if they catch us. But they'll kill you for spite if they find you still here."

She scratched the booty pile, hunting for food. There was nothing save a doeskin bag of spoiled meal, crawling with worms, and a small piece of dried venison, dark and rock hard. Andy tried to take a captured musket. He lifted its terrible weight.

"It's not for the puny," Mary Harris said. Barefooted,

with only the hunk of venison and her child, she started off, taking to the woods instead of the path by which they had come.

"That's not the way," the boy protested.

"They won't look for us so quick in the brush," she said.

Once away from camp, freedom was almost too sweet to bear. They had escaped from the savages at last. Every wild glade looked good. A tiny stream ran across their way, and they lay down on its mossy bank to drink. Before they were on their feet they heard a savage hallooing far in the leafy reaches behind them.

"They come back and found him," Mary said grimly.

Soon the sound of a musket echoed among the hills. A little later, faintly and from a great distance, came an answer, not one shot, but two. After an interval the nearer rifle sounded again. This time Mary Harris didn't speak. Both of them knew what it meant. Whoever had returned had sounded the alarm. His distant companions had heard and answered, telling him they were on the way back and, whatever the trouble, would soon be there to help.

The boy hurried on as best he could. He was still free, but only now did he recognize what a terrible freedom it was, a hundred and fifty miles or more in the wilderness, with no roads, just Indian paths and streams that ran as freely in Indian country as in white, and with signs that could be read only by the savages who had the country mapped out in their minds.

They kept going that day until they could no longer see. That night no painful thongs dug into the boy's flesh, but neither was there the comfort of a fire. He lay close to Mary Harris for warmth and for protection against the black unknown. Not for a minute would he have admitted it to her. He had long since learned not to try to enlist her pity. But just being with her made him feel stronger, and the closer the stronger.

At the first glimmer of light through the trees, they were off, stumbling through the fog-choked woods. As a captive he had had little concern about missing the way. Now their lostness and vast uncertainty in the woods lay on him. But if Mary Harris felt anything, she didn't show it.

"We got sunup to foller in the morning and sunset to keep at our back in the evening. What more do you want?" she said.

Oh, she was a hard taskmaster and let him take no easy way. Once they broke out of the woods into a wild open meadow of coarse grass. It was like coming alive again for the boy, but she plunged him quick as she could into a dense forest of hemlock and pine, where it was dark even by day and the ground lay carpeted with brown needles.

"They won't track us so easy in here," she said.

More than once they came on trails in the forest, not the narrow deer paths that soon petered out. These were wider trails, plainly made by human feet. They looked inviting, a far easier road than over logs and through the brush. The boy would have gladly taken one of them, but Mary Harris would have none of one or the other.

"That's where they'd lay to jump us," she said.

It was late afternoon when they came out on the bushy, bald knob of a hill. This, they could see, was the end of the forest valley they had been traveling since they left camp. Ahead lay two valleys. They couldn't see much, just the wooded openings to each. Now which should they take? Both seemed to lead in an easterly direction. Later they were to learn that only one ran east. The other gradually turned and led south and back to the western wilderness and the Indians.

For a long time they stood ragged and puzzled, trying

to think. Even Mary Harris seemed unable to decide. As they waited, a twittering of birds grew closer in the trees and a flock of red-speckled breasts landed in the bushes about them.

"Why, them look like those same birds that came to our camp," Mary Harris said.

As they watched, the flock, with sudden unity, took wing and flew down the left of the unknown valleys. The boy saw a look of cruel resolve come over his companion's face.

"I listened to them before, and I'll listen to them again," she said, and started to follow.

It turned out to be a rough, discouraging valley, filled with obstructions that boded no good for their choice. The second afternoon the boy said he could make it no farther, not till tomorrow anyway. He was plumb worn out. He lay on his face on a drift of last year's leaves. No, he wouldn't get up any more today. Mary Harris had to lay down her child to yank him to his feet. The moment the baby was set on the ground, it started to squall. The squalling must have sounded a long way through the woods. Far off, they heard an Indian halloo, then an answer from the mountain.

At the terrible sound, the boy got to his feet quickly enough. He trembled so much that Mary Harris had to lead him to a fallen hemlock tree. They climbed its prostrate trunk until hidden in its thickest branches. Settled here for only a little while, they heard the unmistakable click of a ramrod in a rifle barrel. Then all was silent, but they knew that an Indian stood nearby, listening for the first sound to give them away.

More than once Andy had complained on the journey that he didn't care if he lived or died, if the savages got him or not. But now that one actually stood only yards away, it terrified him. Every minute he feared the baby would cry again. The smallest sound or gurgle must betray their hiding place. Hour after hour, Mary Harris sat stolidly with the child pressed tightly against her breast. It slept on, and when it awoke she nursed it. What nourishment it could find in its mother's starved body, the boy didn't know. Never had day held on so long. The savage must have gone, he thought. But when dusk fell thick on the woods, they knew he had been there all the time. Still only rods away, he uttered a terrible yell. Then they heard him leave, hallooing to his distant companion.

Before leaving the fallen tree in the morning, they had the last of the carefully treasured hunk of venison. Black, hard and tasteless as it was, Andy hated to see it go. Now nothing stood between them and starvation. That day they splashed through a swamp where the trees stood gaunt and lifeless above them and the brown stagnant water smelled of death. They chewed the tendrils of the wild grapevines for food and ate what tiny applelike fruits of the wild thorn trees they could find. Of all the country they went through, the thorn-tree thickets were the worst, whipping them, tearing their clothing to shreds, leaving long, bloody scratches on their bodies.

Wherever darkness overtook them, they spent the night, once in a region of rocks, once in a brake of rhododendrons. Hope each morning was soon succeeded by daze and exhaustion. What day of the week or month it was, neither of them had any notion. The morning after the thorn-thicket passage, the boy fell down and couldn't get up.

"You go on," he told her. "Let the Injuns get me."

"You always got to fight something in this life," she said. "If it ain't Injuns, it's something else."

"I can't fight no more," he told her.

She had to take a stick then to beat him up, like the savages did, and after that she wouldn't let him sit down.

"You're worse'n the Injuns!" he cried at her.

"Go holler and bring 'em on. You'll find out who's the worser," she told him.

"You're a devil!" he sobbed at her another time.

"You ain't seen half of me yet," she promised. "Lay down again and you'll find out."

He called her all the mean names he had ever heard. Had he known she was like this, never would he have left camp with her. But nothing he said did any good. She kept driving him on. Just the same, he could tell she was weakening. Her gray dress, long whipped by the brush, hung on her in rags. Her arms and legs and face were bleeding. Next morning, through half-closed eyes, he watched her. After nursing her young one, hardly could she draw herself up by a sapling to her feet.

She can't go far any more, he kept telling himself that day. Then we can both lay down and die together.

Around noon he thought she was ready to give up. She had turned on him a glazed eye. "Listen. Did you hear it?" she asked.

"Hear what?" he mumbled. "I didn't hear nothing."

"I thought I heard a hound," she muttered.

They stood for a time, but the only thing that came to their ears was the sound of the wind in the trees. Could it be she was weak and losing her mind already, hearing things like folks did when they got lost in the woods? Many times after that he noticed she stopped; just the way she stood, he could tell she was listening for the hound she thought she heard. But no voice of a dog came, and none during the night. Morning, when he looked at her, she lay like a dead person, the baby like a bundle of skin and bone in her arms. Then he saw her stir and watched as incredibly she pulled herself to her feet.

Never would they get far from this place, the boy told

148

himself. Then they both saw what they had failed to see in the darkness when they lay down last night—what looked like a wall of logs hardly a dozen rods off in the forest. They stumbled nearer. It was an old cabin with a roof of bark and a window such as only a white man would make. The cabin stood black, fallen in, and abandoned, but never did any house look so beautiful. Then, as they stood staring at it, they could hear, faint and far away through the morning mist, a sound neither of them could mistake.

"Cowbells!" Mary Harris whispered.

Before noon they reached the river. On the other side they could hear the cowbells more plainly now. To the north, blue pine smoke rose from chimneys among the trees. They took a path under the sycamores till they were across from the settlement. They saw a man fishing on the other side. When they called to him, he dropped his pole and ran. Presently they saw him come back with another man. Both carried guns. They got into a boat. Andy thought they were coming to get them, but the boat moved less than halfway across the water. Here it stopped.

"What do you want?" one of the men called.

"We belong over 'ar. We want to git across."

"You don't look white to us."

"I'm Mary Harris from Black Run."

The two men conferred. "You ain't her. She was took by the Indians."

"I know. I'm just a-gittin' back."

"You ain't Mary Harris. I knowed her. I seed her many a time."

The young woman looked down at herself. As if for the first time, she realized she was half naked, her clothes in shreds, her skin dark with blood and dirt, her hair a tangled mat. She looked forty years old.

"I'm her all right. If you come over, I can prove it."

149

"No, we ain't comin' nearer. You might have Indian friends in the bushes a-layin' for us."

"Well, if you won't come over, I reckon I'll have to wade out to you the best I can," she said.

"No, it's too deep!" both men called, but she paid no attention. She handed the child to the boy. She warned him sternly not to let her fall. Then she stepped into the water and kept on till it reached her shoulders and threatened to engulf her head.

"Wait!" one man called. "We'll come a mite closer!"

Cautiously the boat edged toward her. Bit by bit, it grew nearer, until the boy heard an exclamation, followed by others. The boat came faster now, and he saw both men lift the dripping woman in. After that they paddled for Andy and the baby, left on the bank.

Boys must have run with the news, for the far bank swarmed with folks by the time the boat touched shore. Before they got there, the older boatman had taken off his hunting shirt that came halfway to his knees and had given it to Mary to hide her nakedness. Now a man on horseback dismounted to let the exhausted woman ride. Against all these well-fed people, she looked little more than a skeleton, and so must he, too, the boy reckoned, for they lifted him up to ride behind her. Over and over, as the people trooped after, he heard them say how never would they have known her.

In the nearest house they put her to bed. Some of the women began pulling thorns from her feet. They counted a hundred and twelve and laid them on a piece of crockery to show. Others of the women had set to cooking. Now it began to smell good. Mary Harris and the young ones had starved a long time, but their empty bellies would get stuffed with rations now.

It was a man they called Major, in small clothes, his

hair in a queue, who put a stop to it. He came stamping into the house with his cane and smelled the cookery. "What's this?" he thundered. "You'll kill her! And the boy too! The first day you must give them nothing but whey. One spoonful at a time."

The boy hated him. Others would get the venison stew now. But he hated worse the other man who came bursting in the door after dark. All afternoon Andy had been lying on the bed beside Mary, as he had lain beside her so many nights in the woods, but never had he felt such possession and tenderness for her as now when others tried to come between them. She had fetched him out of the woods. If it hadn't been for her, he would not be here. Her face looked almost like a dead woman's on the bolster, but she needn't worry. Never would he leave her. Soon as he was bigger, he would marry and support her.

He felt outraged and affronted when this stranger came and claimed her as his wife. He hadn't even reckoned on a husband. Why couldn't the Indians have got him like they had so many? But no, here he was putting his rough green-and-blue-linsey arm over Mary Harris's breast and her looking up at him like she had never looked at Andy.

"You leave her alone!" the boy said sharply. When some of the onlookers laughed, he turned his face away.

That laugh burned bitter inside of him. He tried to get up and go off by himself, but they wouldn't let him. All night he lay there hating Mary Harris's man. In the woods he had had her all to himself. Now he must share her with this ugly fellow.

Only Mary Harris's babe gave him comfort. The child knew him, had time for him, played with him a little, pulled and fiddled with his long hair. He looked the babe over with lackluster eyes. Anyway, she wasn't married. She wasn't tied up with any man. Should he want to, he might stake first rights to her. She wasn't much as yet, but she was something. If he couldn't have the mother, he might have the daughter—sometime on ahead when she got old enough to have a man.

THE OLD MAN CAME BACK to the present with a start. Where was he? Oh, yes, here in the mansion office. Well, he did marry the daughter, didn't he? There was her picture hanging on the wall. But it was the woman in the other picture who still stirred him the most. He'd never forget her. She was the one to put iron in a man's soul.

As It Was
in the Beginning

WITH THE FEVER BREAKING over him like hot gusts from the burning Jornada, Foard Hudspeth lay on the adobe floor of the little room opening out of his trading post, with his head toward Bent's Fort and his boots toward Santa Fe.

Not yet twenty-four, the form under the rumpled blue-black blanket was long and powerful. His uncut hair reached the collar of his red calico shirt. And the face staring up at the crude ceiling of earth-covered limbs and twigs was strong, even violent, with heavy dark sabers of eyebrows, a face that men might dislike until they became aware of the steady blue eyes and heard the quiet voice and saw him swing unaided a barrel of black St. Louis sweetening from a Missouri wagon.

Out in the trading post he could hear them playing seven-up, could smell the brandy adrip from empty horns at the players' elbows. He kept muttering to himself that he should be out there taking care of his business; repeating in Spanish to impassive Indians the merits of white blankets and sheet-iron kettles; measuring out green coffee and black gunpowder at three dollars the dented tin cup; weighing pelts on the steelyard and dropping the Mexican silver into his clinking keg, which he slept with every night at the head of his *colchón*, with his Hawkins rifle on the floor beside him.

The keg felt almost full again. All winter and spring he traded for a kind of hairy gold, the pelts of wolf and bear

153

and buffalo, with a few beaver, mink and otter still coming in. And summer and fall he traded for wool and oxen and horses and mules, most of which had been stolen in Mexico, but he couldn't prove it.

It was a raw land, rough and violent and rich with opportunity; a land where, if his head stayed cool and hard, the gilt stuck to his fingers, and some day he would build a new post, a store like his father's back in Ohio, with shelves and counters of planed boards from Cincinnati, and luxuries like nails and glass and hinges and sperm candles and quinine and liniment and soap and brown sugar such as most of the people on this side of the plains had never seen.

He knew by his galloping pulse and shortened breath that he was sicker than they guessed out in the post. The voices over the greasy cards kept growing farther away, and a kind of misty light began to creep over the bare mud walls, softening them with familiar wallpaper, and he was back in the gentle, carpeted parlor along the Ohio canal, with his grandfather looking down at him from the wall beside the walnut-framed wreath of his dead sister Cassie. And his mother's white hands lay gently in her lap, while the shaved lips of his father moved sternly in family worship.

But what he could not forget were his five younger sisters, sitting on straight horsehair chairs, all dressed from the same bolt of cloth, none of their shoes reaching the pine flooring, their flaxen hair drawn tightly back from their scrubbed faces. That, he muttered to himself, was all he lacked, not the horsehair chairs or the painting of his grandfather, but the pale hands of a white woman lying in her lap and around him the flaxen heads of his Anglo-Saxon children.

It was queer to come back a thousand miles across the plains to these stolid adobe walls of old Taos that kept watching him like immobile Indian faces waiting for him to die. He wondered how many others they had watched: Mexicans, Indians, Frenchmen, and men from the States, a few who went slowly and peacefully in their blankets, but most of them swiftly, violently, their scalps raining red drops to a thirsty land.

And now the delirium was gathering like a dark, lonely fog about him, and through it he thought he heard as from a great distance his father call his name.

"I'm coming, sir," he muttered.

With effort he rose to his feet and made his way across the earthen floor. It was strange to find it already night in the trading post, and stranger how the talk and laughter utterly ceased as he stood, a tall, gaunt apparition with burning eyes, in the doorway.

He could see them only dimly over their cards: Amasa Smith, whose face was entrenched behind a massive black beard that billowed over his thick chest and who always walked with dignity ten paces ahead of his silent Navajo wife; and small, erect Colonel Pitcher, in baggy broadcloth; and stout, ponderous Ceran St. Vrain, both of whom had married into a powerful native family; and Tom Bibb, a slouching giant in shiny, weather-beaten buckskins, who claimed to have a wife in every Indian nation; and George Sovern, the old man who was looking after the post. And all around them the fire glittered on lead bars and scalping knives and hoop iron for arrowheads, on copperware and brass trinkets and beads, and on a bolt or two of bright red Indian cloth that glowed like spun blood in the shadows.

Tom Bibb took his long legs from an empty keg.

"Feelin' better, ol' hoss?" he threw out cheerfully.

He went on dealing the cards, and after a moment, on the pretext of picking up a dropped card, he rested his huge hand on the other's knee.

"Phaegus, man!" he whistled softly. "He's hot as a hoss-shoe out of the charcoal!"

"I figgered him so," Amasa Smith said through his beard. "He's a sick beaver and he needs a woman to nuss him."

The shuffling and dealing and slapping down of cards went on, but through the haze of tobacco smoke that grew ranker and ranker, and through the blur of Colonel Pitcher's tall, gray beaver hat and Ceran St. Vrain's clay pipe and the staring worn faces of the cards, some of which had been re-marked with ledger ink and Indian vermilion, Foard Hudspeth was aware that in little words and significant glances and Indian signs with their hands, and often in outright sentences, they were talking about him, pitying and yet blaming him that in his years west of the Arkansas he had not attended to the prime duty of every man of taking to himself a wife of the country.

"A woman's a woman," Tom Bibb repeated meaningly, "and when you catch the plague or got the heel of an arrer stickin' out twixt your ribs, even a quarrelin' Blackfoot or thievin' Pawnee got a heart in her."

"Ay," Amasa Smith assented. "And don't forget an Indian woman makes a heap more than a white woman of combin' your hair when ye got it on and a heap louder mournin' over ye when ye got it off."

In the delicate silence that followed, Colonel Pitcher tactfully lifted a burning coal to his pipe.

"There are fine Indian girls," he asserted open-mindedly. "And fine Mexican ones. Hudspeth may prefer the Mexican."

With the fever lapping up in him like a fire gutting a hollow pine, Foard Hudspeth sat on the brandy keg, stiff and silent, remembering how the soft, dark, quarter-moon eyes of the younger sister of William Bent's Cheyenne wife had followed his fringed shoulders at Bent's Fort. And in his mind he could see all the tawny-skinned girls here at Taos who had watched his tall figure at *bailes*, especially Chipita Perea, who had eyes like velvet-black knives and who had once broken an eggshell of perfume over him, shrieking with laughter in front of the crowd. But he had never danced with any of them, only greeted customers and friends and made his way back to the post to smoke by the fire and see girls, whose kind were never seen in this remote land, come trooping through the moving shadows: Rachael Cross, whose brightly beribboned braids used to drag across the front of his desk at school; and Charity Ann Hewitt, who used to sing in the choir and over her sister's cradle; and straw-haired Huldah Baker, whom he had kissed at a husking bee, and whose gentle presence he could still feel snuggled beside him in the hay on a sleighing party to Pyle's Furnace.

They must be all married now, he told himself, living in refined brick or clapboard houses with the sound of the steam whistle in their ears and mirrored in their eyes the peaceful sweep of canal boats to and from Pyle's Locks.

Gradually he became aware of a respectful hush in the post and guessed that the others were waiting to hear the opinion of Ceran St. Vrain, who, with his partners, the Bents, held the esteem of more men, red, brown and white, than any other west of the Missouri.

With difficulty Foard focused his eyes on him. There he sat, wedged in the post's only chair, his great head swimming in wreaths of smoke, his face deeply creased, one finger stuffing fine-cut tobacco and willow bark into the bowl of his famous clay pipe that traveled to Missouri and back again unbroken through hail and ball and whistling arrow.

The fever roared in Foard Hudspeth's ears, but he could hear all that Ceran St. Vrain was sternly telling him: That the Lord Himself had said it was not good for man to live alone; that if his foolish and backward young friend had listened, he would have a woman now when he desperately needed one, a nurse to doctor him with hot herb teas and lay wet cloths on his head. And all this time she would have been cooking him mutton and buffalo jerky, and washing and mending his clothes, and making him at ease and comfortable in his own house.

And now the older trader was resolutely putting his pipe away unlighted and reminding him that he had once been his employer and was still his partner and adviser. And it was his solemn opinion that this very night was the time to say before God and man the name of the woman he wanted, whether Chipita Perea or an Indian girl from the pueblo, or a Navajo, a Kiowa or a Ute. And if God made him well again, then he could not very well put off this necessary part of life. And Padre Martinez could marry them. And the coming Christmas there would be a woman in his house as there should long have been.

Through the dense tobacco smoke the other men nodded vigorously, but Foard Hudspeth was remembering the last white woman in his eyes, some girl watching the teamsters load the mountain of bales to the sheeted wagons at Independence, and not until he had crossed the plains among all these black-maned women had he realized how fair that girl's hair had been there in the Eastern sunshine with all the settled states across the sandbars of the Missouri River behind her.

He heard his own voice like a stranger's in the post: "What you say is likely, Ceran. I am needing a wife and I've been thinking about one I've never seen. You'll know her name. I mean the one with Shaved Head's tribe these years."

"Shaved Head?" The older trader spoke in slow and profound distrust.

"He means the white girl, I take it," Tom Bibb put in,

his gray eyes keen on Foard's face. "The one that was took from the wagons."

Foard could see them all peering at him thoughtfully now through the growing dimness. Smoke was drawing through pipes and mouths, and he knew they were darkly remembering—Pawnee Creek; the Krider emigrant train on the California trail; two Pennsylvania wagons far to the rear, cut off, with the rest of the train looking helplessly on; all that was left of the wagons, black seared spots on the grass; and the two small boys and a girl of twelve galloped off in front of rawhide saddles with the hair of their father and mother and older brothers dripping blood back into their childish faces.

"She's good Comanche now, I'll warrant, if she ain't rubbed out," Amasa Smith muttered.

"Ross, her name was, if she remembers she had a white name." Ceran St. Vrain's round face was bleak. "Charles told me her hair was white in the sun. But the fort could never close a trade with Shaved Head."

"I'll trade with him!" Foard said steadily.

The next thing he knew was a hearty hand clapping him on the shoulder, and Tom Bibb declaring that a yellow-haired Comanche ought to make a wife, and Amasa Smith grunting that the young beaver was human and a man after all, and Colonel Pitcher insisting they drink a toast to the pair. And presently someone stuck a horn of brandy into Foard's unseeing hand and Colonel Pitcher called on them to stand. Then all Foard knew were the sickening fumes of brandy over the front of his calico shirt and oblivion rising like forked black lightning from the earthen floor to meet him.

He had the dim memory of climbing alone through a dark pass in the Raton Mountains from the top of which he would see the horned tepees of Shaved Head's village with the sun shining on a Comanche girl's yellow hair. But the winding pass never came to an end, and whenever he stopped, there were armed Utes with furs to trade for powder and ball until his body was piled with pelts and his feet could scarcely drag.

He awoke wringing in perspiration, lying on his *colchón* in the familiar room, with nearly a dozen layers of blankets piled over him. Out in the post he could hear the old Yankee voice of George Sovern droning in Ute: "I'll give you a knife and a sheet-iron kettle and all the beads you can grab in your fist." And sitting here on the floor between him and the fire were the old Mexican midwife, Juanita, and Hoska, the toothless Navajo slave of Ceran St. Vrain, watching him unwinkingly from black eye-holes in their wrinkled masks.

A little later he heard Juanita's Spanish from the gallery.

"He get better now," she informed some *compadre*. "Already he look like a man who think about getting married."

Lying there on the floor Foard had just been thinking that only a week ago a white woman in his house was as far from his life as the steamboat whistle at Independence. And now before the week was over, the daughters of Trinidad Garcia were cleaning out the rubbish and sweeping his floors and patio, and whitewashing the dingy walls, and covering the ceiling with bleached muslin from his shelves. And Navajos were coming to trade their rugs to make soft stepping-stones on the adobe floor and subtly reminding him how a Comanche woman would be fond of red. The *carpintero* had promised the two handmade chairs with tall backs like a bishop's and a great bed wide enough for two, like that of Padre Martinez. And every day there was one customer or another to answer if it were true that the hair of the woman coming to live in his house was the color of ripe barley straw and, now that she had lived so long with the Comanches, would she dress in deerskins or calico, and would she eat with a fork and spoon or dip into the bowl with her white fingers?

They left with everything in the house in its place and Foard in his saddle, his six-mule wagon piled to the sheet with square stacks of pelts for William Bent to sell for him in St. Louis, and a small chest packed with his ceremonial suit of blacktail deerskin, long broadcloth trader coat, and gray cassinette trousers. Across the square the two Bent and St. Vrain wagons waited to join them, and Tom Bibb, a guard as far as the fort, was throwing his long legs and rifle over the back of a scrubby dun.

"Pay my respects to the bride!" Colonel Pitcher called from his doorway.

When Foard looked back, the leaves of the town cottonwoods were delicate with spring on the upper Rio Grande, the brown walls of Taos were rosy-golden in the sun, and chattering brown women in blue and black *rebozos* were pointing out to nearly naked children the unridden mare tied to the rear of Foard Hudspeth's wagon, a mare with a ewe neck, a coat like a worn mocha glove, and the gentlest, surest-footed mount for a woman north of Chihuahua.

But what Foard remembered chiefly was the corpulent figure of Ceran St. Vrain standing in the doorway of his post, smoking his clay pipe, his eyes clouded and his usually cheerful countenance grave with thoughts unspoken.

All day Foard could see him as the rims of the two wagons cut broad tracks up into the mountains that shut Taos off from the rest of the world. They climbed through forests of the Utes and Apaches, where the trunks were black, cinnamon red or silver gray. They rolled through a lofty canyon where the world was still white and buried with winter. They came down with locked wheels into spring again where a broken-down ox branded with a large B was feeding along the stream. And they climbed still another range that was the outer wall of Taos.

"Thar your Comanche girl be!" Tom Bibb said, swinging the long barrel of his rifle across a land larger than Ceran St. Vrain's La Belle France, where the cedar foothills below them rolled into gray sandhills that bordered a sea of grass sweeping endlessly eastward until the rolling green waves washed up on Missouri farmland.

For ten days horses and wagons had crawled the crude trail from Taos. Now as they rounded a bend of the Arkansas, the weary mules freshened. Tom Bibb's scrubby dun in front pricked up its ears and nickered, and Foard, who was riding beside him, saw the familiar adobe walls rising like a medieval fortress across the river.

Today as always when he came on the place, it was a faint surprise to find it here on the homeless plain, surrounded by unseen savage hordes, not an Army outpost, but the private enterprise of a few businessmen from the States, the only established settlement between the Missouri and the mountains.

Two hours later Foard was in the clerk's office, a room hung with the dusty gifts of the chiefs of the Cheyennes, the Arapahoes, the Kiowas, and the Comanches. William Bent, a slight figure with an indomitable chin, dressed in his usual chief's buckskins, talked of the winter trade, of the price of furs, of friends who had lost their scalps since fall, and asked for the news from Taos to Chihuahua. Then he filled a long-stemmed pipe.

"Your message came and I sent it to Shaved Head. My Shawnee found him camped on the Little Clarita. I've been feeding three of his men since Monday. But," he concluded laconically, "the girl is dead."

Out in the fort Foard could hear the squaw wife of one

of the teamsters quarreling in shrill Cheyenne. It ceased and in the sudden quiet the patter of half-breed children scampering overhead on the fort walls was like the bare feet of his unborn, yellow-haired children running out of his life. But his face did not change.

"You believe a Comanche, sir?" he asked.

"It's the Comanches who say she's still alive." With a determined face, William Bent kept striking steel and flint until his tinder blazed and his pipe was going. "My Shawnee never saw her. Four years back I heard Shaved Head had killed the Ross boys because they cried too much, and I tried to trade for the girl. The next winter Shaved Head sent word she was sick and he wanted to trade her before she died. I sent him a small part of the goods he asked for and promised the rest when he brought the girl. He never came in. His tribe hasn't been near the fort since."

Foard was silent until he saw an answer was expected.

"You know Indians better than I, sir," he said quietly. "But if the girl was sick or even dead and they wanted to trade for her, I'd never expect them to say she'd been sick. And if they said she was sick, I'd expect her healthy enough or traded at some other post."

William Bent eyed the younger trader.

"You're shrewd, my lad. This is your trade, and I'm going to let you trade it. But don't forget that when you deal with my friend Shaved Head, you're dealing with the craftiest fox on the prairies."

He rose, and together the two men walked out into the gravel courtyard. Three Indians, their moccasin tassels dragging the ground, were coming through the tall, open gates of the fort, short men, looking shorter off their horses, a squat figure in the lead, elk's tooth on his neck, heron's plumes in his hair, and a brass-bound fusil in his hands; the others in flaps, their bare copper shoulders slung with buffalo-hide quivers. And in their step was all the arrogance of men who held the whip hand in what was to come.

"I'll talk to them out here," Foard said, his jaw tightening. Straight, tall and uncompromising, he stood waiting for the trio to mark him out and come to him, which they did unerringly. "How?" he said without emotion and shook hands.

"How?" they said, and their sharp black eyes appraised him from head to toe.

Half-French and half-Shawnee, Marcellin Le Crouse stepped up to interpret, a strip of calico plaited in his dark hair.

"Tell them," Foard began impassively, "that I hear the squaw with the yellow hair is dead."

The faces of the three Comanches grew stolid at the translation. The squat one lifted from around his neck a small pouch of beautifully worked doeskin. Without expression he slowly unrolled the soft leather and suddenly there in his dark, greasy claws was a lock of the yellowest hair Foard Hudspeth had ever seen. Soft and light, it caught the sun and diffused it like threaded gold until the young trader's face grew bleak with suppressed emotion.

"How do I know it wasn't cut from a Comanche scalp pole?" he asked harshly.

The courtyard had grown very still. Up on the walls pacing men with rifles had halted. Even the half-blood children playing over the buffalo robe press had frozen at the words. And all around him Foard knew that in the shadows of the posted gallery men and women had drawn from work and living quarters to watch and listen, stocky French-Canadians, silent Shawnee and Delaware hunters, a few tattered Missouri volunteers, the black-bearded missionary to the Utes waiting to return to St. Louis, swarthy Mexican helpers, weather-beaten trappers who carried in their heads a vast unmapped empire, and bearded wagoners soon to set out on the yearly Bent and St. Vrain caravan to Missouri, most of them married, their listening squaws in leathern wrappers and leggings, their Mexican wives in short red cotton skirts, and not a woman among them with skin lighter than buckskin.

"How does the young white chief know," Le Crouse translated in Comanche, "that the hair wasn't cut from a Comanche scalp pole?"

Slowly there in the sunshine as the insistent answers came and the savage hands pantomimed, and with the lock of Anglo-Saxon hair in his fingers, Foard could almost see her, a sturdy, blue-eyed figure in deerskin skirts, brushing back her heavy yellow braids as she dressed a staked buffalo hide or raised a tall Comanche lodge or fetched a horse and fastened the rude rawhide saddle for her lordly Comanche father.

"If the yellow-haired squaw is still alive," Foard asked quietly, "why doesn't Shaved Head bring her to the fort to trade?"

The black eyes of the squat Comanche glittered, but all he said was that the growing age of Shaved Head kept him from making the long journey to see his friends in the lodge of the white men, and if the young white chief journeyed to the Little Clarita, Shaved Head would bargain with him for the price of his daughter.

Foard's face did not change.

"If Shaved Head's daughter with the yellow hair still stays with the Comanche people, tell her to send a message of what she used to do when she was a girl back in the white man's country. Then the young chief from Taos will come to the Little Clarita to trade for her."

Long after the hoofs of the Comanche horses had splashed silver in the river, Foard stood on the wall smoking and watching the three dark specks vanish into that wilderness south of the Arkansas. And he was up on the broad top with his pipe the evening that lance butts pounded on the great doors studded with nails and sheet iron. When Bent men called down, it was the squat Comanche with a dozen warriors to escort the young white chief to Shaved Head's lodge on the Little Clarita. A lance from someone on horseback was lifted up in the starlight, and Foard found hooked to its point a roll of blue drilling such as might make a chief's saddle blanket.

Silently Foard unrolled it and held the cloth to the faint glow of his pipe. Staring back at him from a dark background sewed with firm white doeskin stitches he read the words: "Ursula Ross," not printed, but written in a girl's round, upright hand like the name of his mother on her yellow sampler back in Ohio.

They left in the early morning, Foard and Tom Bibb on their saddles and Le Crouse with a pair of pack mules and the gentle, ewe-necked mare tied behind. And when they looked back, the brown walls of Bent's Fort were like a toy fortress on the prairie.

For days they saw only the black smear of buffalo to the east, and twice smoky herds of antelope floating like the shadow of a desert cloud across the prairie. Then suddenly in the twilight they topped a long, grassy ridge and saw below them in the wide *cañada* the horned lodges of a Comanche city of noble proportions with a semblance of streets and cross streets and all the life and movement of a white man's village.

Foard had pulled up his roan at the sight. Sitting there on the saddle he could hear rising to his ears the laughter of squaws, the distant shouts of naked red children chasing a yelping pup, and the chatter of dusky maidens coming with leathern buckets to the stream.

166

As It Was in the Beginning

"I kinda wish, ol' hoss—" Tom Bibb confided.

He broke off oddly. For a moment there were only the murmur of the tepee city and the notes of a love flute in the twilight. Then Foard heard it again, drifting through the wild peace of the evening, that incredible, long-unfamiliar sound of a white girl singing. Faint, faraway, more like a dream to the ear than anything else, but with an indescribable emotion in this unaccustomed savage place, it floated through the moist air that hung above the river.

> *"Come, ye disconsolate,*
> *Where'er ye languish."*

Slowly, as it went on, it gathered strength and serenity, and something far back in Foard Hudspeth's blood caught in his veins, and whenever in later years he was to hear the stately movement of the hymn, he could see the whole scene rising in front of his eyes: this lonely *cañada* in the wide solitudes, dotted with the pronged lodges of the Comanche, with the soft flow of the prairie stream reflecting the evening clouds and the village fires' deep scarlet, and the green range dotted for miles with herds of grazing horses and mules under the eyes of nearly naked sentinels who sat their mounts on the ridges like burnished bronze statues against the wide circle of the sunset.

Then the little party rode down into the *cañada* and splashed through the stream, and the cry of their coming echoed ahead in the village, and standing in front of the largest lodge was a powerful figure in only a pair of leather breeches with tassels on the welt, his chest bare and scarred with wounds, his head shaved on one side to the center, the other side bearing a long queue that, plaited with buffalo hair, fell to his knees.

"*Côm' estamos?*" he greeted them briefly in the Mexican

vernacular, his face bland as a copper idol; but the eyes in that wrinkled skin were the blackest, boldest and most cunning that Foard had ever seen, eyes that had looked unmoved on birth and death, battle and dancing, and on other things that few white men cared to see or remember.

Then he pointed to the pack mules and spoke a few words in Comanche.

"He says," Le Crouse translated, "is that all you bring? He expect he see white man's wagons heavy with goods."

"Tell him," Foard said coldly, "the white chief didn't come to trade for ponies and buffalo robes, only for a squaw with the yellow hair."

The chief grunted and led the way into the big lodge that smelled of native sumac-leaf tobacco shot through with the sharp, ammoniac odor of burning buffalo chips. No white girl waited in it. And no one came into it that night but a squaw bringing food in a wooden bowl, and another who had taken care of the horses, throwing down the bridles, and as the evening went on, a procession of village dignitaries who quarreled for their proper place in the circle according to their rank and then sat there smoking the white man's tobacco, a glitter in their eyes for the young white chief and his packs bound in gray wagon sheets and piled in the rear of the lodge.

All evening no mention was made of the girl. Long after the lodge was quiet for the night, Foard lay awake watching the fire wax and wane and the white smoke curl like spectral fingers over two of Shaved Head's youngest children sleeping with dark disordered hair over their faces, and listening to the village dogs bay at the black silhouette of a thousand lodge prongs against a yellow Comanche moon.

Then quietly he made up his mind to trade for the girl in the morning and turned over to go to sleep. And the bubbles of firelight running up the lodge poles were the red flashes of mountain cedar on the freshly whitewashed walls of the post at home. And the breathing of one of Shaved Head's squaws in the lodge was the breathing of his own wife with yellow hair sleeping for the first time in years in a bed, a large bed like that of Padre Martinez, big enough for two, in his own house at Taos.

When he awoke, Shaved Head was gone on some mysterious tribal business. He did not come back that day or the next, while Tom Bibb spat with growing distrust, and the expressionless Le Crouse hummed a monotonous Shawnee dance, and Foard grew more taciturn as he played euchre on a blanket or walked around the village. But all he saw were old squaws over pots and hides, and younger squaws plaiting horsehair ropes and rawhide lassos, and the young unmarried squaws dashing expertly about the *cañada* on their trained horses while the Comanche beaus, vainer than any white youths, rode and strutted in front of them with small trade mirrors and vermilion-painted faces.

The fourth morning Foard spoke sternly to the squat Comanche message-bearer: "Ask Shaved Head if the young white chief is a small boy playing dice with polished plum stones that he is kept waiting three days and nights. Say that in Taos he is a man of business, and every day red men, Mexicans and white men come to trade with him. For many suns he has been on the journey to Shaved Head. Now he wants to return to his people."

Late that afternoon the squat Comanche brought word that Shaved Head would speak on the council ground in the morning, and Foard could feel the wave of suppressed excitement that ran through the village. When he awoke, Le Crouse and Tom Bibb were ready to carry out the packs, and Foard pulled on his ceremonial shirt of blacktail deerskin, tasseled and fringed, collared with beaver and worked with beads, porcupine quills and squares of black velvet.

When he stepped outside, the white lodges of the Comanche city were red in the first rays of the sun. Not a squaw was in sight, but the scourge of the prairie squatted in a rough circle under mantles of red and blue strouding and woolly buffalo robes. No one spoke when Shaved Head appeared, walking slowly and with great dignity from the lodges, flattened silver and gold coins tinkling from his ears, an old dragoon sword and scabbard buckled around his waist. He did not offer to shake hands, but stood, austere and aloof, among his people.

"The white chief," Foard said gravely, "waits to hear Shaved Head's price for the squaw he is so ready to return to her people."

"Can a Shawnee," the chief warned, "understand a Comanche when he talks long and fast in council?"

"The chief has only one mouth that I can see," Foard answered. "And the Shawnee has two ears."

Shaved Head's eyes glittered. He made no reply. For a long minute those ageless eyes wandered among his hearers. Then slowly he began to speak. He recited how as a young man he had been a comfort to his father's old age as the greatest horse-stealer in the Comanche nation, how as a warrior in his prime he had taken more scalps than the young white chief could lift in his hands, and that now as an old man only the mention of his name made the hair of the Osages, the Lipans and Pawnees tremble. He boasted how he had never attacked his white brothers from concealment like the cowardly Apaches, but slaughtered them fairly out in the open, and how his heart broke for the white nation, which was why he consented to give up his yellow-haired Comanche daughter, for whom the young fops of his tribe made tweezers to pull every hair from their faces and bodies, and who, if she stayed, would some day bear his tribe warriors with the cleverness of the whites and the horsemanship and bravery of the Comanche.

As It Was in the Beginning

The rich young chief from Taos had asked the price of the squaw with the yellow hair, and now Shaved Head would tell him—a herd of fast horses and mules, and many swords and rifles for the Comanche to protect himself against the Mexican, and a wagon of blankets so the tribe could sell its buffalo robes to the traders and still keep warm in winter, and tea-kettles so that all over the village they could sing the Comanches' love of peace and brotherly affection for the white men.

These were only the beginning of Shaved Head's demands. On and on for more than an hour, growing more imperious and arrogant with every breath, the old orator thundered, the words pouring out faster, the flattened coins on his ears jingling, his scabbard rattling and flashing fire. And every few minutes he thought of some fresh grievance and demand. And all the time Foard sat with unreadable face and unmoving figure, while Tom Bibb's blue eyes grew bleaker and Le Crouse had ceased monotonously to hum.

When the speaker finished, scores of eyes glittered with amused mockery for the young white chief who thought he could trade with Shaved Head. Then Foard rose, and it was plain that he had made his decision.

"Be sure, Marcellin," he said sternly, "to say exactly what I say, no more or no less. Tell Shaved Head I have heard his eloquent oration and his price for the white squaw he loves so much and wants to give back to her people. Tell him he has asked for anything and everything he knows he can't get except the moon to hang on one lodge pole to light his tepee at night and the sun to hang on another to warm it by day. Tell him that when I can give him the sun and the moon, then I will also give him all the other things he asks for."

The translation into Comanche was followed by silence broken only by the children and dogs in the village. Foard went on: "Tell Shaved Head that I am not a miserly man.

For this squaw with the yellow hair, whom I have not yet seen, I am prepared to pay a good price—three Navajo blankets for Shaved Head's favorite daughters, and three copper kettles that shine in the sun, and ten plugs of tobacco, and ten rounds of brass wire, and a bolt of Choctaw stripe that brightens the squaws' eyes, and a bolt of blue drilling like the sky, and six abalone shells that will make many pearl buttons, and a rifle, not like the Indian carries but like you find in the white man's lodge, with a long arm that talks here in the council ground and finds the heart of a deer across the river, and a bag of powder and ten bars of lead, and a sack of the white man's coffee that every Comanche likes. And there are more buffalo robes than there are suns from summer to winter."

Shaved Head spoke with great dignity and contempt.

"He say," Le Crouse droned, "a Southern Comanche already poor from two wives offers more than the rich young white chief for the squaw with the yellow hair. Now he tells the Comanche bring him what he tie to Shaved Head's lodge last night in the Comanche custom."

A Southern Comanche with tattooed face and chest rose and swaggered swollenly across the circle. He came back leading his saddled horse. Hanging from his bridle were the bear claws of a mighty hunter, a cloth-lined scalp, the symbol of a brave warrior, and a mule's tail to show that he was an illustrious stealer of horses. And strung out behind him, lifting their heads and snorting at the red crowd, were eight or ten fine unsaddled horses with bright calico plaited through tails and manes, all of them groomed from ears to hoofs and shining in the sun and bearing the large markings of Chihuahua and Durango brands.

Shaved Head grunted with satisfaction, and the eyes of the circle glinted as always at the sight of Comanche gold.

"Shaved Head say," Le Crouse translated, "can the young white chief give a more better trade than this?"

As It Was in the Beginning

Deliberately Foard walked around the horses, scrutinizing them. Then quietly he spoke to the Shawnee: "Cry around the village and council ground. Tell them the white trader has fine goods to trade for fine horses." When he turned, Tom Bibb had already begun to loose the rawhide knots and lay back the worn gray wagon sheets of the packs.

For several minutes the savage circle sat unyielding. An old one-eyed warrior was the first to break away. At the sight of him standing over the open packs and fingering the long rifle, others came. And in time most of them were there, talking rapidly to each other and calling for their squaws. And presently the *cañada* about the village had become a scene of great activity with the roping of horses, and the council ground was like a love feast with squaws and bucks swarming with horses, first the poorest, and at last the better, with Foard looking into their mouths and pulling their tails and standing tall and inscrutable while the owners ran their animals up and down. And every brave, squaw and child in the village seemed to be there with eyes glittering at the horse fair. And Tom Bibb's face had brightened and Le Crouse was humming some Shawnee love chant under his breath, and finally the packs had grown nearly empty and Foard had a *bayo* coyote with a dark stripe down back and legs, and a fleet-looking *grullo*, the color of a sand crane, and a dappled *palomino* with white mane and tail, and a black-maned buckskin, two or three pintos colored like bolts of crazy calico, a tall black without so much as a white eyelash upon him and a *sabina* stallion with pink muzzle high above the crowd.

Then a scar-faced Comanche came riding bareback on a lumpish, churn-legged horse with a rough coat like an old sheep, but there was no laughter in Comanche eyes. The crowd fell back gravely to make a long aisle on the council ground, and the scar-faced rider passed like the wind. And Foard knew that here was a horse that would seal any bargain. He threw all the remaining goods on a pile and pointed to the horse, but the Comanche held back craftily.

"He say," Le Crouse translated, "young white chief don't have anything Comanche want."

"Get me what's left in the last pack," Foard said, and when Le Crouse handed it to him, he pulled off the wrapping of an old, moth-ravaged buffalo robe, and the sun glistened on a brown jug with a bung of pine wood forced into its mouth.

Tom Bibb's eyes were a bright blue again and Le Crouse hummed a Shawnee dance under his breath, and the scar-faced Comanche was coming up eagerly with his horse. But the wrinkled face of Shaved Head had gone suddenly black. All through the horse-trading he had sat on the ground, composed and aloof, watching the dealing and bargaining with no more expression than a heathen god. Now he was up on his feet, his blandness had vanished, and he was rattling sword and scabbard in a fury. And Foard could see what his face had been like when he rode toward the enemy in battle, and he was pouring out a flood of sharp Comanche words that cut like lance points. Children were scattering, and squaws and braves, including the scar-faced owner of the sheeplike horse, were falling back like cattle.

"Shaved Head say," Le Crouse translated quickly, "he don't need the horses. He got plenty horses. He's an old man and don't want more horses. He tell them give back the goods in the Indian custom and the white man give back their horses."

In a minute the irate old chief was making straight for Foard, who stood tall and unshrinking while a torrent of words he did not understand poured over him.

"Shaved Head say," Le Crouse told him, "the young white chief's tongue is split. He don't say he got a jug of Taos brandy to trade for the squaw with the yellow hair."

As It Was in the Beginning

"Tell Shaved Head," Foard answered, "the jug didn't come to be traded. It came as a present to help Shaved Head forget the loss of his Comanche daughter."

Shaved Head stood for a minute or two gazing at Foard with unfathomable eyes.

"In the morning," he said harshly, "the white chief can go."

It was late afternoon when the packs were knotted again in their rawhide thongs and carried back into the big lodge, and much later when the three men from Bent's Fort joined the other sleeping figures radiating around the small fire in the center of the lodge like spokes in a wheel.

When Foard awoke, it was daylight, and Tom Bibb was sitting up on his robe with an expression that told Foard something had happened. Quietly he turned his head.

It was a young squaw. She must have risen early and entered soundlessly in her moccasins, and now she sat cross-legged on the ground just inside the closed flap of the door. In the dimness of the lodge she might have been a Comanche sitting there in her scalloped deerskin skirt and leggings, a necklace of lead pellets at her throat, a rude copper bracelet on her arm, one hand above the other in her lap, silent, as if she could sit there all day without moving, her half-closed eyes on the ground, her only show of emotion a faint trembling of her eyelids when Tom Bibb cleared his throat with awkward feeling.

Then Le Crouse threw back the buffalo-hide flap of the door, and Foard told himself that as long as he lived he should never forget the picture of the sun streaming into the lodge over Ursula Ross, her stoical cheekbones, and her shining yellow hair falling to the ground in two thewlike braids. When Foard spoke to her, she looked up, and at the sound of the English words, something deep and unutterable, almost terrible, flooded her eyes. Only for a moment. Then they were gray and Spartan again, and Foard had the feeling that if no white men had come to the Little Clarita, she would have walked straight and silently the Comanche trail laid down for her.

"I don't talk the language of my mother for a long time," she told him. "But every day I sing so I remember."

Squaws brought the white men's horses, the mules, and the ewe-necked mare with the surest hoofs north of Chihuahua. From over the village, Indians had silently gathered. The young squaws ran up and rubbed red cheeks against the white cheek of Ursula Ross. The squat Comanche with the necklace of elk's teeth was there with a dozen mounted men, all smiling broadly. And Shaved Head came slowly and heavily out of his lodge.

"The packs wait for their owner to open them," Foard said to him.

The old wrinkled face did not change.

"The white chief from Taos wears a Ute hunting shirt. But underneath he is a Comanche. When the grass is green another time, I come to Taos to trade and see the face of my Comanche daughter. Now your brothers take you safe to the white man's lodge on the big river."

From the crest of the grassy ridge they looked back on the Comanche lodges standing so white and lonely in the *cañada*. Before the largest cone a bare-chested figure raised a hand. Foard raised his. Then village and *cañada* were swallowed up in the rolling wilderness behind them.

The Arkansas River was red with another day's sunset when they drew up their horses to wait for Tom Bibb before taking the water. From somewhere hidden in the dusk on the other side they could hear the movement of a late traveler on the trail. It was only a familiar rattle and clatter, but the girl's face tightened and her hand trembled on her bridle rein.

"It's a wagon!" she said with suppressed emotion.

As It Was in the Beginning

Behind them Tom Bibb rose in his stirrups, patted a huge hand to his mouth, and a long, undulating yell of savage greeting echoed up and down along the bluffs of the river. And when they reached the tall, nail-studded gates of the fort, William Bent himself and his Cheyenne wife stood in the gateway with the population of the fort scattered behind them or strung along the top of the wall above.

It was good to come into settlement life again, a walled settlement with a dining room that had tables and benches, knives and forks and tin dishes; with lighted candles by evening, the ring of blacksmith and wheelwright hammers by day, and day and night the salt of short English words sprinkled on the air. And every hour or two it was good to look up at the living quarters of the Bents on the wall and to know that Ursula Ross was up there being cared for after her long bondage.

The third day they called Foard into the clerk's office, and William Bent was there in his hickory chair with his chin tucked obdurately into his buckskin collar.

"It's your Ross girl, Foard," he said. "The missionary's been up talking to her. Talking to me too." He twisted uncomfortably. "Did the girl tell you she'd marry you, Foard, and go along back to Taos, or did you take it for granted?"

Foard remained strained and silent, and William Bent's chair legs screeched painfully on the adobe floor.

"Dammy, Foard, you can buy a squaw, but you can't a white girl. Not even out in this country. She's got to have a chance to go back East to what kinfolks she's got left if she wants to."

The younger trader stood in a kind of stunned rigor as if the Arkansas had suddenly stopped flowing and for a hundred miles around the fort antelope and buffalo had frozen to the plains. But his face did not change.

William Bent rose and crushed a centipede on the floor.

"She wants to talk to you. She's up there now with the

177

missionary and Mrs. Bent." Then, as if he knew what was coming and was anxious to get as far away from it as possible, he went out across the courtyard toward the small gate that led to corral and blacksmith shop.

For a long time after he had gone Foard stood there in the office watching the air from the left-open door stir the black feathers of a long Kiowa lance that hung on the wall. Then he walked slowly out on the gallery and knew that William Bent wasn't the only man the missionary had spoken to, because Tom Bibb came up with a disgusted look in his hard blue eyes.

"Let's me and you go back to Taos, ol' hoss," he said.

It was strange how, at the giant's words, Foard's post on the ancient adobe square came back into his mind like a picture of home. He could see it plainly as if he were there, a thick candle burning on the rough counter and flickering on dark ropes of tobacco, on black gunpowder and gray bars of lead, and on bolts of Indian cloth that glowed like spun blood in the shadows. And all around the table, sprinkled with cards and brandy horns, the peaceful pipe smoke hovered over familiar bearded faces.

"I have a little business to tend to first," Foard told him.

When Tom Bibb had walked away, he looked up at the flat-roofed room of the Bents on the wide wall. He told himself that sooner than go through what waited for him up there, he would run the length of a Pawnee gantlet. But gradually around him on the posted gallery he could feel the eyes of Tom Bibb and other men covertly watching him. His cheeks went a little flat. Then with silent steps he climbed the plank stairway and knocked on the paneled door that had ridden a wagon a thousand miles before it had ever ridden a hinge.

William Bent's Cheyenne wife opened it. Her copper face was stoical, but her eyes glinted.

As It Was in the Beginning

"*Num-whit,*" she said and held back the door.

Tall and almost as gaunt as that night with the plague when he had stepped into the post, Foard went in. Rolled mattresses to sit on stretched along the wall on the floor. A pile of unwashed wool lay lightly in one corner and William Bent's tall butternut secretary, surmounted by a stuffed eagle, stood heavily in another. There were a stove Foard doubted if the Cheyenne woman ever used, a table with water bucket and dipper, and two chairs, one of which held the black-coated missionary smoking a short pipe.

But what stood out before all the rest was the girl, still in her scalloped deerskin skirts, sitting there quiet and composed as if she had sat on chairs all her life, and behind her, as though she were trying to shield it, a large leather trunk, probably the one William Bent had taken in trade for oxen from the Mormons last summer, its lid thrown back, and scattered over it a dark cashmere dress, a ball of folded white stockings, and a pair of ladies' black boots.

When she saw who it was, the girl sat straighter, and tiny invisible strands of strain tightened in the room. Then she rose and pushed her chair toward him as she had probably seen William Bent do, and Foard told himself that she was quick to learn as a steel trap.

"Sit down," she said in a low voice.

"I'll stand, thank you, ma'am," Foard answered gravely. "I have an idea you won't need me much longer now."

A faint color stained the girl's cheeks. She stood facing him, and he had never noticed before how straight as a lodge pole she was. Deliberately he forced himself to look away and stare hard and long at the missionary, who refused to take the hint and go, but sat there calm and pious, the puffs of blue smoke escaping at regular intervals from his black beard, his eyes keenly fixed on the girl's face.

Foard suddenly realized the girl was talking to him, in

short, difficult English sentences that still had a little of the singsong flavor of the Comanche squaw.

"I asked for you to come up, Mr. Hudspeth. I had something to say to you. I thank you for all you did for me. You are a good man."

Foard's face remained unmoved.

"But not good enough," he said with quiet bitterness, "to go to Taos with to live?"

"I didn't say I would go to Taos," the girl testified quickly. Her gray eyes flashed. Her rounded cheekbones stood out like small, unyielding rocks, and Foard could see that here was a woman you couldn't drive.

"No." Foard's voice was without emotion. "But you knew I came to the village to trade for a wife, and you didn't say you wouldn't go with me then."

"I didn't see you then," she said. "I didn't talk to you till the trading was over. Besides, I wanted to go. I'd have gone away with any white man. They killed my mamma and papa. They killed my brothers. I'd have done anything to get back to my people."

The missionary took his pipe from his mouth placatingly.

"I'm sure you won't lose anything on the transaction, Hudspeth," he promised. "Miss Ursula had the storekeeper make out a list of what you paid Shaved Head. She says when she gets back East, she'll bind herself out and send you the goods before she marries another man."

Foard utterly ignored the missionary. The girl took a folded paper from her deerskin bodice and handed it to him, then sank back to watch him from the chair. His fingers unfolded the paper and he ran his eyes over it. The storekeeper had done a good job. It was substantially correct. But a deep red color had crept up into his throat and face.

"You don't need to bind yourself out to pay anything to me," he told her harshly.

As It Was in the Beginning

The girl leaned forward with intent gray eyes.

"Are you saying I'm free now? That I can marry who I please, like other white women?"

Foard couldn't look at her. He told himself that she kept putting her finger on the spot that hurt. And now the freshly whitewashed walls of his house at Taos came rising in his mind to plague and taunt him, the new Navajo rugs on his floors, the two chairs with tall backs like a bishop's, and the bed wide enough, like that of Padre Martinez, for two. And he could see in his mind all the people in Taos whispering among themselves that he had come back alone.

For a long minute he stood there breathing hard. Then his fingers tightened, and the sounds of tearing paper ripped through the silent room.

"Now you're free as any other white woman," he said. "Marry whoever you please."

He turned toward the door. Before he could lift the latch, he heard a man's voice speak in low Ute.

"If she's a white woman, why don't you ask her to marry you like a white woman?"

Foard stopped heavily and looked around. The pious, black-bearded face of the missionary was unchanged, the blue smoke still coming in peaceful puffs from his lips. And William Bent's Cheyenne wife was watching him and the girl with a suppressed something in her glittering dark eyes. But Foard, standing tall and rigid, knew that these would be the hardest words that he had ever tried to say.

"You can go back East if you'd rather, Miss Ursula—" he began painfully.

There was the clean lift of the high prairies in the girl's face. She had risen from the chair, and the sun through the window caught her left braid, turning it to a rope of gold. She was waiting for him to go on. But Foard heard the door close softly behind them; and when he turned, the missionary had left and only William Bent's Cheyenne wife stood there watching them with greedy but strangely softened eyes.

Long after the gates were locked that night, Foard came out into the dark gallery, tall and restrained in his white cambric shirt, long trader coat and gray cassinette trousers. He heard the growl of moved tables in the long, low dining room and was aware that deep in its warren of living quarters and earthy passageways the fort was coming alive. And after a while doors around the square began to open and dim figures slipped in twos and threes and whole families across the dark courtyard, in mute moccasins and hard-heeled boots, in whispering buckskins and deerskin skirts that tinkled with small bells, necklaces and brass bracelets. Men laughed and Mexican women chattered in excitement, and the scent of Taos brandy darted like lizards along the moist layers of the evening air.

Then suddenly the yellow square of light in the room up on the wall went dim. A tin lantern holding a candle appeared at the door. And three figures descended the open stairway—William Bent, his slender legs twinkling under the tails of a coat he wore to St. Louis; his Cheyenne wife in bright Choctaw stripe; and a strange white woman with yellow hair, in a Mormon's dark flowered dress with wide white bands, a slender waist, and full billowing skirts that she held up with both hands so she wouldn't trip on the stairs.

It was strange that Foard scarcely remembered the ceremony, only the utter steadiness and gentleness of the white woman who stood by his side. But never afterward could he hear the tune of "Money Musk" without seeing the long cave of the fort dining room, with tall candles of buffalo tallow wildly aflicker, and fiddle bows sawing, and swirling through the haze of rising adobe dust two score of frontier dancers celebrating the wedding; bearded wagoners in freshly washed, check linsey shirts gravely swinging their Mexican wives until their short red skirts flared above dark knees; and lanky hunters and trappers, their buckskin fringe flying, kicking up their moccasined feet and whirling their wooden-faced squaws in all the steps of the fandango and contra dance, the rocking war dance and slipping gallopade, and the rough, boisterous pitching of Missouri backwoodsmen.

The Dower Chest

I<small>T'S JUST A RELIC TODAY</small>, a huge old box, plain and ugly as sin, with a heavy and unwieldy lid. The date, 1762, when probably it was made, is carved crudely in the dark-stained pine. Those who pass it in the museum scarcely give it a glance. Of what use is such an ancient and monstrous thing in this modern world? they think. For never in those early times did folks have such terrible problems to solve as today.

But if you wait till the guard has wandered into another room, you may, if you are strong enough, lift the heavy lid. And in the breath of vanished old quilts and early American life rising from the grain of wood you may catch the faint scent of hickory smoke and May apples that clung around the dress of Jess Galloway, the bound girl, as she stood that day of the mid-Revolution in the tiny settlement of Fisher Valley and faced what the future held for them all.

Oh, she knew what awful thing was wrong with the world, and had known it for some time. Men in a hurry had been stopping off in the settlement on their way south. What they said was told only to the men behind closed doors, but you could leave it to the women to find out. And when they had, they wished they hadn't, for this wasn't just an Indian scare. No, this was extinction, the end of the world for central and northern Pennsylvania, and perhaps much farther. The enemy was leading the savage to burn, scalp and exterminate. In all this great empire of forest, no white men or women were to be left alive.

Ever since spring, settler folk had been driven out, but now, with the terrible news from the Wyoming Valley of Pennsylvania, those still left were a-clearing out their own selves. That was a sight to see, men, women and young ones in boats, arks, canoes, rafts—anything that would float, even hog troughs—a-running down the Susquehanna! Most of their farm and household stuff had to be left behind. And this was only the west branch. It was the same on the north branch. Where did all the displaced settler folks come from? Jess wondered, for these were just the lucky ones that got away. Behind them in clearings for many a mile folks lay with woods flies a-buzzing at their hacked heads and at the brains of their littlest ones busted against trees.

But do you reckon the men in Fisher Valley would go? No, not them. They said the Dunkards on the other side of Third Gap in Limestone Valley weren't going at all, and Fisher Valley would wait till its crops were harvested. Even then it would be hard enough to give up the good black land they had cleared and the log buildings they had raised. Their flax they would have to leave unpulled, and their corn stand small and green in the field. But their wheat and rye they could reap, thresh, sack and tote along. It would give them bread this coming winter wherever they might be.

Now today the last of the wheat was being flailed, and tomorrow they would go. Hardly could Jess believe that this was their last day in the valley. Seldom had she seen a seemlier one. The air from the English Lakes blew clear and crystal over Shade Mountain. The July sun lay golden on the long, ragged wheat stubble. Blue dinner smoke rose from the small cluster of clay chimneys, and the gray walls of the settlement looked as soft and homelike as guinea fowl.

But where was Ashael? All morning Jess had asked this of herself. Here it was the last day and no sight of the stern young Amishman who last spring had asked the elder to marry them. The elder could have done it, too, for it was given him to baptize and marry as well as preach. But he wouldn't set Jess free till her contract was up. You might think Ashael would get mad, so straight and small and doughty he stood, with a blue eye like ice in his sightly face framed by his red hair and beard. But the Amish were men of God, and more patient than this one looked. All he said was he would wait, and went back to his bachelor improvement over Shade Mountain.

This morning, threshing on the barn floor, Jess kept going to the door. But never did she get a sight of his clean black suit, fastened with hooks and eyes, and his blacker hat with the broad brim.

"If it's Ashael you look for, you needn't," the elder told her at last. "He's not coming."

The bound girl felt the flail strike against her heart. "Didn't you send him word?" she cried.

"Oh, he's plenty word. Not for anything but God would he leave this place, he said. You ought to remember how stubborn he is. Not a penny would he pay to buy off your contract. Not even to marry you."

"Why should he?" Jess stuck up for him. "He's just starting out, and poor."

"Not so poor. He has the Great Chest from the old country. But he wouldn't part with it."

"What would be the use? He can wait two years and get me for nothing."

"Yes, if you stay single for him. But how does he know some other man won't come along and buy you off from me? You're big and strong and a good worker. Some even say you're good to look at. Women don't grow on every bush in this country."

"Ashael don't need to worry. I'll wait for him," Jess said stolidly.

Just the same, hardly could she eat her early noon dinner. In the middle of it a Tioga man with long hair and a boy on the saddle in front of him rode out of the woods shouting terrible words. He halted by the elder's house and called that Dunkardtown in Limestone Valley had been burned. All were wiped out. Wasn't there some saved, Jake Bender asked. Not a Dunkard lifted his hand or complained, the stranger said, for that was against their belief. "It's God's will," was all they said as the tomahawk fell on themselves and their families. Of the whole settlement, only this boy he found hiding in the woods was left to tell him what happened.

Everybody in little Fisher Valley had crowded to hear and sicken, everybody save Jess. All she could think of was Ashael alone over in his valley. None saw her, except it might be Mary, as she put the house between her and the people. By the run, her feet fell on the Indian path across the mountain.

Many a time when she went for the cows or on a Sabbath walk had she thought of her marriage day when she would take this path to Ashael's valley. First the path led through a wide hollow of noble pines and hemlocks. Even in winter the snow looked dark in here. Beyond was the spring where the great velvet bird's-foot violet and yellow lady's-slipper grew. Oh, this path would be a mortal sweet place to walk on your marriage day, but today she saw feathers in every bush and a spear in every sapling.

So thick stood the forest on the north side she could get no look at the valley below. Not till she reached the bottom, had waded Ashael's creek, and climbed around the limestone outcrop did she come out in the clearing. There stood the peaceful scene like always. Ashael's log cabin, his round-log barn, his stumpy fields in wheat, grass and corn, with a patch of potatoes by the house. From the woods came the lazy tank-tank-tank of a cowbell. The wheat stood uncut, for the season came a little later over here. In the hayfield loading his cart was Ashael.

His horse, lonesome over here in this valley, gave a little whinny at the sight of Jess. Until then, Ashael didn't see her. That was Ashael all over. The savages could crawl within a dozen yards of him and never would he believe they were there. He looked for good, not for evil. But he was the man for her, Jess told herself, seeing him again standing there by his cart so straight and doughty for such a little fellow, and mighty brave to be living by himself over here in the wilderness.

His face hardly changed as she told him about Dunkard-town. His eyes kept looking around his little farm in the clearing. She hardly believed that he heard her. His strong cheeks kept warding off the bad words, so that it seemed even to Jess what she said couldn't be. The hay smelled tame and sweet like always over here in this peaceful valley. Wheat stood gold as a sovereign on the stalk. A bird sang mighty pretty in the forest, and over them stood the mountain like a sentry on guard. Only the ugly recollection of what the Tioga man had said kept coming back to plague her.

"Don't look at your crops, Ashael!" she begged him. "Just go before it's too late!"

"Run off, you mean?" He looked at her sharply. "Where can you go from the hand of the Lord? He can strike you down in Lancaster town as easy as up here."

"He kin," Jess agreed. "But most likely He won't want to. Now I can't say that much for the Injuns."

"No red man would do me harm," Ashael promised. "Not a one ever left my door without something to eat or a place to sleep."

"That's what the Dunkards used to say, and look what happened to them!"

189

"It was the Lord's will," he said, very low, but Jess heard him.

"The Lord had nothin' to do with it," she declared warmly. "The Dunkards just wouldn't stand up and defend themselves."

"It's in our Bible. If your adversary strike you, turn the other cheek."

"You don't always git a chance to do that with an Injun," Jess observed. "Once his tomahawk hits you, you're a gone Josie. You got to hit him first."

"Our people," Ashael said, "don't take up arms against anybody."

"Wouldn't you lift a hand to save your own self . . . or me?"

"No, for to lose your life is to save it."

Jess looked at him. "Then it's true what Elder Kring said about you."

"What did he say?"

"That you were stubborn as a mule."

"I'm glad if I'm stubborn in my belief."

"Well, if you want to be stubborn, I kin too," she told him. "It says in the Bible it's not good for man to be alone. And if you won't come with us, I'm a-goin' to stay up here with you."

The first alarm crossed the Amishman's face. "No, that you can't do."

"Why can't I? Who'll stop me?"

"I will," Ashael promised. "Never will I live with a woman in sin!"

"It would be only for a year or two," Jess explained. "When a parson comes through, we kin be married. If none comes, we could go down the river sometime . . . once our young ones are old enough."

"That's enough!" Ashael cried, and his face was dark

with anger. "Till your time is up, you belong to the elder! If you won't go back yourself, I'll have to take you!"

Jess's mouth got a peculiar ropy look, and if Ashael had known her better, he might have taken warning. But at that moment rumbling sounds rolled along the mountains, as of distant thunder.

"You ought to git your hay in first, Ashael," she said mildly. "I kin help you. Then you kin send me over."

"How do I know," he asked sternly, "that a girl who would live in sin will keep her word?"

"You're a man," Jess said, still meek as Moses. "And if I wouldn't, you could make me."

"Yes, well," Ashael agreed. "If you want to help a little, Jess, I won't say no. Afterward, I'll walk with you over the mountain. I meant to go over anyway and give everybody good-by."

The rest of the day, scarcely speaking, they worked in the hayfield. Jess raked the hay into piles and stood on the cart to stamp down the fork-loads from Ashael. Sometimes she took the fork her own self and swung up as heavy loads as he. She believed she could lift still heavier, but never would she shame Ashael in his own field. It took longer than they reckoned. When they finished, the sun was already down behind North Mountain. The valley felt cooler in shadow. But where was the storm whose thunder they had heard? The sky still hung without a cloud and blue as a gentian.

"Hadn't we better milk before we go?" Jess asked, still mild. And when the milking was done: "Ashael, I'm a mite hungry. I guess it's from the hay and crossing the mountain. If you feed every savage that comes this way, maybe you could spare me a bite of supper. It wouldn't hurt you to eat either."

He gave her a searching look, but did not refuse. Sitting

there at the hewn table in Ashael's cabin, with Ashael's own bread and milk between them, with his fireplace on one side, his gun, that must be used only for game, in the corner behind the door, his bed on the floor, and near it the long chest that came from the old country, Jess felt almost like already she was Ashael's wife and mistress of his house and lands. Never, she told herself, would she give him up now. First she would put him off till tomorrow. Then the elder and the Fisher Valley folks would be gone.

So long did she keep sitting at the table after Ashael finished that he grew uneasy and restless. He got up and put away all save her bowl and spoon. Now with impatience, he watched her make what little she had left last a long time. Daylight faded from the cabin, so that already it seemed dark in here.

"I have seen many eat, but never a bird like you," he told her at last. "How do you get any work done?"

"I kin work with any woman!" Jess shot at him. "Or with a man either!"

"Then let's see how good you climb the mountain," he said, "or it will be dark on us before we get started."

She pushed back her bowl and spoon. "It's no use, Ashael," she said. "I'm not a-goin' off without you."

She was not prepared for the terrible look that came on his face. "So the word of a girl that would live in sin is not worth anything after all?" he lashed her.

"I never said I'd go . . . only that you could make me," Jess reminded.

"So I could . . . if I wanted to," he rebuked her.

For a minute they faced each other, Jess with her black hair and slate-gray eyes, and Ashael with his red beard and hair and his eyes blue as limestone. He stood so straight and righteous for such a little fellow. Oh, he had muscles you could never pinch. He could give her a tussle, if he

192

wanted to. But in her heart Jess knew that never could he throw her and drag her out. No, rather she could swing him off the floor and set him where she wanted.

"Only my belief stops me," he said, bleak as a plowed field in winter. "You needn't worry. I won't lift my hands against you any more than against an Indian."

He went to his long chest and began lifting out what lay inside. He made all into two piles and tied them up in the blankets from his bed. Then he went for the door.

"Where are you goin', Ashael?" she asked.

"Not with you, woman," he said. "If you won't go from here, then you can stay and I will go. The Indians can't drive me off. Only one like you can. If you come after me, I'll leave where I am and go up to Dunkardtown."

"Dunkardtown is burnt, Ashael."

"Not the land. A new house and barn I can build for myself."

Quietly she sat at the table. Presently she could hear him out at the barn, hitching up and throwing his farm things in the cart. He drove to the door and started to carry out his packs and kettles.

"You needn't do that, Ashael," she said, getting up. "I only reckoned to stay and help you with your work and cook your meals and sew your clothes. But I won't run you off your own place. If you won't stay, then I'll go my own self."

"You said that before."

"I'll go for sure now," she said. "Good-by, Ashael."

"Wait! I want to go along and see that you do what you say!" he said sternly.

"You needn't. I gave my word now."

"I'll go just the same," he told her. "You could hide in the woods and come back tonight or tomorrow. It has neither bar nor lock on my door."

Well, it was all over, Jess told herself, as they tramped up the mountain. Likely this was the last time that ever she would see him or cross Shade Mountain. It was pitch dark when they reached the summit. The moon would soon be up, Ashael said, and then they could see, once they got out of the timber.

"You're sure they didn't leave this morning already?" he asked of a sudden, when they were halfway down.

Oh, she knew what made his suspicion. She noticed it herself—the smell of smoke; not the good homelike scent of chimney smoke, but the rank stench of burning household logs, chinking and rubbish. It grew stronger as they went by the dark spring, through the black pines and hemlocks and by the unseen swamp, where the cows liked to get away from the flies. Then suddenly they came out of the woods and saw in the darkness before them great red eyes winking at them from where the settlement ought to be.

"Ashael, don't go any farther!" she warned him.

Ashael had stopped, but only for a moment. "I'm not scared," he told her. "Nobody will hurt an Amishman. But you better stay back. I can't answer for you."

It was true, Ashael feared nothing, she told herself, as he went on, with her following close behind. Her eyes could barely make out the path in the meadow they followed. Halfway across, Ashael stumbled over something, and she thought she heard him take the Lord's name under his breath. When she reached down, her hand froze. Here in the path she could feel a dress and apron she thought she knew, but the body diked out in them lay stiff and cold.

"Ashael!" she cried, stifling a scream. "It's Mary!"

Ashael stood by with a man's clumsy sympathy. She could not see his face, but he did not take off his broad-brim hat. "God's will be done," he muttered in the dialect.

Huddled there above the silent body of her friend, Jess

waited while the story of this shocking thing worked like a deadly poison through her mind. The savages must have struck that afternoon not long after she had gone, and that had been the rattle of distant thunder that she and Ashael had heard. Likely Mary had run for the mountain, too, and here they had overtaken her. In her mind's eye Jess could see a savage with his uplifted tomahawk cutting her down.

For a while longer she and Ashael stood there, listening, watching. Not a shadow moved across the dying red beds of coals. No sound rose save the hoot of some big-eared owl up the valley. Where the settlement had stood and flourished with human life and household comforts, and with shelter and feed for the stock, now all was death and desolation.

When he started on, she came after. She remembered the saying of Jake Bender that seldom the savages attack at night. No, they preferred to do their dirty work in the day-time and camp by evening in some hidden spot far from their bloody deeds. Just the same, she would have felt better with Ashael's gun in her hands. When they reached the ashes of the elder's barn, no rifle cracked or arrow sang, though they stood plain targets against the scarlet-orange embers. As they stayed on there, the moon came up, lately full, bulging a little on the side, as if misshapen with the evil of the night. Rather she would have had it down, for now they had to put their eyes on what there was to see.

One by one, they accounted for all of the settlement save three. Tilly Fegley they found lying on her face, scalped; and Mordecai with his wounded head in the spring that still flowed a little red, Jess fancied. Jake Bender was a mutilated sight and the reason plain to see, for his gun, with the barrel bent nearly double, lay by the ashes of his house. His wife and old mother were behind the wall of the barn, and Sairy lay in the garden, her sunbonnet hanging on a scorched bush of little dark-brown blooms that the

Pennsylvania Dutch call shrubs. The Tioga man and the boy on the front of his saddle must have gone before the attack. Not a trace of them could be found, or of the two small Fegley boys. Likely they were taken prisoner, for young whites make as good Indians as red ones. But where was the elder?

Then, as they came to the walnut by the run, a figure with gory head sat up and asked for a drink of water. He was a fearful sight to see, like somebody rising from the grave. His eyes already had the glaze of death, and when Jess ran with water in a broken pot, he had lain back again and barely could he swallow.

"Where are the others?" he whispered.

"They are here," Jess told him.

"Gone, all gone," he moaned.

"All save the Fegley young ones," Ashael said.

"And they are worse than dead," Jess added bitterly.

"Well, I am not long for this world either," the elder said, very low.

"You'll be better by morning, perhaps," Ashael promised.

"Don't fool yourself, Ashael," the elder whispered hoarsely. "Don't wait too long, like we did."

Ashael didn't say anything.

The elder went on. "One time you asked for Jess. Now I give her to you. She's no good to me any more."

Jess saw Ashael flinch.

"She must go down the river, elder," he said. "We are not married."

The elder lay awhile breathing heavily, his pale eyes fixed on one and then on the other. "You want him in marriage, Jess?"

She turned slowly and looked at Ashael. "If he's a-willin'," she said.

196

The Dower Chest

Together, she and Ashael waited. The elder lay for a while with closed eyes. They did not know if he was dead or dying, but then he looked at them.

"In the name of the Father, the Son, and the Holy Ghost!" he began in a voice so strong it startled them. "We are gathered together for the purpose of holy matrimony—"

That was the strangest wedding Jess Galloway ever knew, with never a house or room to be married in, with nothing but the night air to stand in, with the holy words said by a preacher cut down like a tree on the ground, and with the moon for light, while around them still glowed the evil embers. One time the voice of the dying elder rang out like that of God Himself, and then again it grew so faint that Jess had to bend her head to listen, for never would she miss hearing the words of her own marrying. But the worst was that Mary and Sairy couldn't be with her at her wedding.

She was Ashael's lawful wife now, she told herself when it was over. It put iron in her as she went around with him fetching the bodies in to be buried in the elder's root cellar. Never could they dig a separate grave for each this night. Here they could lay them all side by side, with the oldest at one end and the youngest at the other. Many times Jess went over their order in her mind, so she could tell where each lay. They had no box, but Ashael spread over them some bedclothes stiff with blood that had missed the fire. Then Ashael, with the pick, and Jess, with the shovel, caved in the earthen roof of the root cellar and covered them over with the dark, rich soil. Not till they were done did Jess come on freshly cut grass and leaves covering a spot of ground. When they bared it, they found a new grave. Ashael said it was an Indian grave, and if they dug, likely they would find the savages accounted for by Jake Bender.

It was late, and the bulging moon half-gone across the

sky, when they started back to their place in Ashael's valley. Rather would Jess have gone for the river, had Ashael been willing, but she was a married woman now, and where her man went she would have to follow. Oh, never, when she thought ahead of marrying Ashael some day, did she expect such a sober wedding journey as this over Shade Mountain in the dead of night, with the lonesome feeling that in this vast region they were the only white people left alive.

Her first word she spoke when they came to the summit. "Ashael, do you reckon you could do something for me and count it a weddin' present?"

"If I can, Jess, I'll do it," Ashael promised. Never had his voice sounded kinder.

"Will you put a bar on the door tonight when we git home?"

He was silent awhile, and she knew she had displeased him. "I'll do it, like I said, if you want me," he agreed. "But it can do no good. Those who come by my house are always welcome, and I'd have to open the door anyhow."

Jess felt thunderstruck. "You mean you'd open to those red devils?"

"Their skins are red, but they have souls like we do," Ashael reproved her.

"Yes, souls black as the pots of hell!" Jess told him. "They'll never come in my house!"

"Then I'll have to go outside and talk to them."

"After what you saw tonight?"

"They did a bad thing, and I don't stand up for it," Ashael said. "But 'vengeance is mine; I will repay, saith the Lord.' Anyway, they would never do it to me."

"But what if they did?" Jess demanded.

"Then it would be God's will," Ashael said humbly.

Jess's face in the darkness was bitter. In her heart she prayed that Ashael's barn and house might be burned down when they got there. It would mean that the savages had come and gone. If the house and barn stood, it meant it was still to be. Oh, never for a minute did she expect that they would be overlooked. The savages knew every white place north of the mountains. Not an improvement but was marked in their minds for destruction.

Her prayer was not answered. When they came up the cart path, around the shale bank, and into the clearing, there stood the house and barn in the moonlight exactly as they had left them. The ax raised up undisturbed from the chopping block. From the barn came Gruzel's whinny, and from the woods the lazy tank-tank of Star's bell. The moon itself hung peaceful far up the valley, throwing long shadows over the fields. Only the black stumps made her think of savages a-hiding in the wheat. She picked up the ax from the chopping block and took it in with her. Inside the cabin, once they had lit a fire of hickory bark for light, all was tranquil and untouched.

Was it possible she had been wrong? she asked herself. Could it be that those red heathen would not bother Ashael, knowing his ways for peace? Then she forgot her fears, for this was her wedding night. . . .

It was getting daylight when she awoke. Now what had awakened her, she wondered. Then she heard it again—an anxious whinny from the barn. Jess got up swiftly and went to the open window. A morning fog covered the valley, but it was not heavy enough to keep her from seeing a file of three figures coming, silent as the mist itself, from the woods. Almost she gave a cry of joy, for the first looked like a woman in a red-check gown. With a flash of warm feeling, it came to her that no longer was she the only white woman in these lonesome woods. Today she would have another of her kind for company. Then the joy died in her throat as she saw that the figure carried a rifle, like the others, and that all three had the same tufted and half-shaven heads. Suddenly she knew, with a wave of horror, where she had seen red checks like that before—in a tablecloth from some Pennsylvania Dutch settler's house, now likely in ashes and its mistress murdered close by.

"Ashael!" She tried to rouse him. As the file of men came closer, her eyes tried to make out what besides rifles they carried. Furry objects, they looked like, some short, some long and flowing, some black, brown and fair as tow. Now she recognized them for what they were—scalps stretched over hoops to dry, and perhaps the freshest was the long chestnut hair of Mary Bender.

"Ashael!" she begged, and touched him, but his breathing never changed from the long, deep snores that all night had seemed to suck up the air around her, so there was none left for her to breathe. Oh, she knew men were heavier sleepers than women. Mary used to say that her father would sleep through a thunder-and-lightning storm. But this man of hers must be the master sleeper of the lot. Or else his work of yesterday, the strain last evening and, on top of that, his wedding night, had been too much for him. In his red frame of beard, his sleeping face looked like a saint's, but one that even in his dreams knew his own will and would suffer none to change it.

She looked around. The great dower chest still stood open, its lid back against the wall as Ashael had left it last evening. She bent down and slipped her strong young arms under his back and knees. The rhythm of his breathing changed for a moment. Surely now he must get awake. Then, after a lick, his snores rang out stronger than ever, as if to drown out this interference. She lifted him quickly over inside. His knees had to stick up. His snoring had stopped now. She set a chip on the chest's edge for air and closed the lid. Then her fingers fastened the iron catch with the peg.

Now, God forgive her, but there Ashael would have to
stay. In her bare feet she went to the door and braced it shut
with a puncheon. As she straightened she saw a curious-
looking stick moving beyond the window. It pushed higher
and closer to the sill. Then she knew it for a bruised and
splintered ramrod sticking out from its thimbles. A greasy
rifle barrel and painted face followed, both turning this way
and that, trying to find the Amishman in his bed.

Jess's hands were slowly fixed on Ashael's gun standing
by her in the door corner. An ancient and heavy piece, the
fore stock had been fastened to the barrel with bands of
tow. Whether it was loaded or not, Jess did not know, only
that Ashael's other gear he kept in working order. This gun
might never be used save on game, but if she knew Ashael,
it would be primed and ready. She cocked the hammer. At
the click, the savage looked up and saw her in the dimness.
Before he could turn his rifle, she drew a bead on that paint-
streaked face and pressed the rusty old trigger.

The roar echoed through the cabin. Then, as the sound
kept on, Jess realized it wasn't the shot any more, but a
violent pounding inside the chest.

"Jess!" Ashael shouted. "Let me out!"

She paid him no attention. The savage was gone from
the window, but now she heard them at the door. Oh, that
was the savage way—to draw a white man's fire and then
get him with the tomahawk before he had time to reload.
Jess threw down Ashael's gun, for it was no use to her now,
and set her stout body against the door, with the ax beside
her.

"Jess, live you yet?" Ashael called. "Let me free!"

"I live yet, Ashael, but I can't let you free!"

"Woman, open this chest!" he ordered in anger.

Oh, if Ashael wasn't a godly person, if only he had been
one to quarrel and fight, like Jake Bender, she couldn't have

opened the lid quick enough. If ever she needed a man by her side, she needed him now. But not a lover of peace to open the door, hold out his hands, and then all he could say was, "God's will," when a bullet fetched him down. Rather have him stay where he was. That's why she had put him there. And yet, how could she hold the door herself against three? Already the puncheon was beginning to slip in the earthen floor. She could hear the savages' fearful yells of exultation as they felt the door give. In violent jerks and shovings, they pressed it far enough for one with his hatchet to worm himself a little way through, and another to put his head after.

With her strong foot and thigh wedged against the door, Jess held them there. Ashael's ax hung clenched in her long, powerful fingers. Now her face grew cruel and the memory of what pitiful things she had seen last night steeled her arms and heart. Sucking in her breath, she raised the heavy bit.

"That's for Mary!" she cried, when she fetched it down. "And that's for Sairy!" she cried louder, as she struck again and kept on till both lay like butchered bullocks between hewn door and log jamb. Then, taking a fresh hold, she waited for the third. But although she stood there a long time, none came. She opened the door a little wider. The mist had thinned. After a while the sun rose over Shade Mountain. The clearing looked calm and peaceful in the light. She could hear the sound of water running over stones in Ashael's creek. Over and over again came the mortal sweet song of the wood robin.

Not till then did she think of the window. It flashed through her mind that the other savage could have reloaded and shot her in the back while she stood there. But when she went to the window, she saw him lying on the ground.

The loud rattling of the chest roused her. Well, she had done what she could. She guessed she must let Ashael out now. Much rather she wouldn't, for it would take a braver body to stand up to Ashael than to the savages. Making a sober face, she pulled out the peg and laid back the lid. She knew then she wasn't wrong, for his face was like the avenging angel's when he came out. Not a word did he say to her, even after he saw the savages at the door. In silence he took the gun and ax, and carried them out to the barn. When he returned, it was with the shovel and grubbing hoe.

Long before he came in, she had breakfast ready, and he ate his fill, but not a word could she get out of him. His face was grim as stone. Oh, she had time now to think over what she had done to him. She had lifted her hands in arms against those who came to his house. She had saved him, but she had disgraced him too. More than once had she heard of a Swiss or Dutch wife who bedeviled her man till he made a vow never to speak to her again. Not for a minute had she dreamed she would do such a thing to Ashael. She should have known better. Never need she expect him to open his mouth to her again.

That's the way it worked out. Corn ripened, was cut, and husked. Snow fell and melted. Ice formed on the gats. Snow fell again, and this time it laid. Now, wasn't it too bad? They were two that had been spared from the heathen, maybe the only two for a hundred miles, and here they had to live together like dumb brutes in the stall! When he sat with her at their table, it was like he had no tongue. Even his prayers to his Maker were dumb. Only his lips moved.

Well, if he would say no word, neither would she, not even about the babe she carried. When the pains came on her one night in April, never did she let on. She got his breakfast like usual, though hardly could she wait to get rid of him from the house. The young one gave her a hard tussle before it was born. More than once that morning she would like to have called to Ashael for help, but she set her jaws tight. If he could take care of his business without talking, so could she. More than once she had helped with birthing. Now she tended to herself, crawling to the fire on her hands and knees for warm water to wash the babe, to smooth it down afterward with melted coon tallow, and for the child's long flannel gown she had long since sewed with Ashael's coarse thread and needle.

Back in her floor bed, Jess lay with her babe close by her. Well, Ashael could hold his tongue from this hour if he wanted. She had a man now she could talk to and listen to. Already he was telling her things at the top of his Tom Thumb lungs. If Ashael wasn't plowing in the far field, he couldn't help but hear him.

Toward noon, when the babe slept, she was startled to hear somebody talking. It must be Ashael talking to the horse, she reckoned. Then she heard voices she had never heard before—white men's voices. They sounded from the barn. After a while she could tell they were coming toward the house, for it was noon and time for dinner.

Not soon would she forget how strange and shy she felt when the soldier stepped into the cabin. Why, he was the first human being, besides Ashael and the baby, she had laid eyes on since early last summer! Behind him came another. Both carried muskets.

"You didn't say you had a baby!" the first one called out.

Jess saw Ashael reach out his head at that. Oh, never a word did he say, but a look spread on his face that Jess never saw before and hardly ever after. He stood for a shake not knowing what to do, and this his own house and household goods. Then he came over to the bed, and Jess saw him watching the little old puckered red face sticking from the bedclothes beside her.

"It's a girl or boy, Jess?" he asked very low.

"It's a boy."

"You all right?"

"I'm real good."

"Can I get you anything?"

"No, but I reckon you'll have to git your own dinner," she told him.

That's all he said and that's all she said, but never would Jess have believed the good feeling that ran over her. Ashael had talked to her. Nerve strings she never reckoned she had in her body let go. The cabin took on a different look, like it had the first time she laid eyes on it. Through the window she could see the bright sunshine on the red flowers of the maples. Down in the gats peepers were calling.

Ashael got dinner, with the two soldiers helping. All the time they swapped news. Their talk sounded sweet as music in Jess's ear.

"We never expected to find somebody living up here," the first soldier said. "I still can't get it through my head. How was it the Indians didn't get you?"

Ashael thought a minute. He looked over at Jess, and his face was sober as a dominie's on Sunday. "It was the will of God," he said shortly.

A Note About the Author

CONRAD RICHTER was born in 1890 in Pine Grove, Pennsylvania, the son, grandson, nephew and great-nephew of clergymen. He was intended for the ministry, but at thirteen he declined a scholarship and left preparatory school for high school, from which he was graduated at fifteen. His family on his mother's side was identified with the early American scene, and from boyhood on he was saturated with tales and the color of Eastern pioneer days. In 1928 he and his small family moved to New Mexico, where his heart and mind were soon captured by the Southwest. From this time on he devoted himself to fiction. *The Sea of Grass* was awarded the Gold Medal of the Society of Libraries of New York University in 1942. His celebrated trilogy, *The Trees* (1940), *The Fields* (1946) and *The Town* (1950, winner of the Pulitzer Prize) make up *The Awakening Land* (1966), a film of which was telecast by N.B.C. in 1978. *The Waters of Kronos* won the 1960 National Book Award for fiction. His other novels include *The Light in the Forest* (1953), *The Lady* (1957), *A Simple Honorable Man* (1962), *The Grandfathers* (1964), *A Country of Strangers* (1966) and *The Aristocrat*, published a month before Mr. Richter's death in 1968.

A Note on the Type

THE TEXT OF THIS BOOK was set on the Linotype in a new face called Primer, designed by Rudolph Ruzicka, was was earlier responsible for the design of Fairfield and Fairfield Medium, Lintoype faces whose virtues have for some time been accorded wide recognition.

The complete range of sizes of Primer was first made available in 1954, although the pilot size of 12-point was ready as early as 1951. The design of the face makes general reference to Linotype Century—long a serviceable type, totally lacking in manner or frills of any kind— but brilliantly corrects its characterless quality.

Composed, printed and bound by The Haddon Craftsmen, Scranton, Pennsylvania. Typography and binding design by WARREN CHAPPELL.